I0731767

USA TODAY BESTSELLING AUTHOR

ALLYSON LINDT

Chapter One

My friends and my business were the two things I loved most in this world.

They were also currently the two things causing me the most frustration. I was heading to my favorite all-night bookstore—could it still be a favorite if it was the only one?—in an attempt to take my mind off both.

I wasn't sure I could enjoy the trip through my guilt, though. I'd blown off my friends' invitation to spend time with them and their guys, by telling them I had to deal with my shop. Now I was here instead.

For years the three of us were Sadie, Anne, and Lyn. Three Musketeers. Peas in a pod. All sorts of cute phrases for things that just fit perfectly together. But things had changed since they landed themselves in long-term relationships. It wasn't that they'd cut me out of their lives, but each of the was with two men, and most of that group consisted of our inner circle. Hanging out with them meant watching the flirting, the googly eyes, and subtle intimate touches. And now I was Lyn The Third Wheel. Seventh wheel? Either way, I was the spare, in the trunk for emergencies, but otherwise, on the outside looking in.

That analogy was crappy on a lot of levels, but no one was around to hear it, so I wasn't going to fix it.

I wouldn't wallow, though. They were happy, and I was genuinely glad to see that. Sometimes I just wasn't in the mood to be immersed in their gooshiness.

All right, I was a teensy bit jealous that they each had two guys. I'd never had a problem getting laid. It was easy to hide my insecurities and extra pounds behind a mask for one night, but longer than that and both became evident.

Not wallowing. Not wallowing.

My night would be filled with enjoying a good book, and coffee made on someone else's espresso machine.

The bookstore-slash-coffee-shop was nestled in a part of Sugar House where old and kitschy met new and trendy.

This was one of the original buildings in the area, and I loved the way vines crawled along the stonework outside. Inside had a similar feel, with solid bookshelves extending in every direction, and an eclectic collection of wrought iron and carved wood in the café.

asking for it

I liked to wander when I came in here. There were certain sections I always hit up—romance, sci-fi fantasy, and manga—but I wanted to stroll past all the books, make sure I didn't miss any or leave any lonely.

There were people in almost every aisle, reading, browsing, and lingering. It was a gorgeous sight.

I'd stay in the stacks for hours if I didn't have to be up early in the morning. I wanted to buy everything that caught my eye. With all my spare money going back into Java Loading, my anime gaming café, I had to limit myself to only a few books.

Selections in hand, I paid, and made my way to the adjoining coffee shop. They had a new salted caramel, extra espresso, with a mocha whip drink that looked incredible.

And it was probably a billion calories. I got the no-caff, no-sugar, no-fat macchiato instead.

There was one free table left. Score. I took my drink and settled in to read. The chatter washed over me, making the scene in my book, where the heroine meets the hero in a crowded train station, feel more real.

"Excuse me," a seductively deep voice said.

I glanced up from my book to find the owner of the voice watching me with starkly pale green eyes framed by black hair. *Hello, sexy.* "May I help you?" Some nights I might flirt with him, but I wasn't in the mood tonight.

"I'm Fred, this is Barney." He jerked his thumb at the guy with him. Who was just as gorgeous. *Fred* looked more professional, in a button-down shirt with the sleeves buttoned around his wrists, and *Barney* was in a faded concert T-shirt and battered jeans.

The serious one and the clown. Interesting, but not unique, combination. Stupid names. "I'm Betty." I could play along with whatever their game was until they were gone. Especially for the view.

"Told you she was a Betty." Barney nudged Fred. No surprise, Mister Concert T-shirt wasn't as reserved, but he was just as nice to look at as his friend.

Fred pursed his lips, but turned a smile back on me. "We're sorry to interrupt. There are no more free tables. May we share yours?"

It was a polite enough request. I gestured to the chairs next to me. "Help yourself."

Fred nodded at my book. "It must be a good book."

"It's one of my favorite series." It was the new issue of *Spring Popcorn*. The artwork was Japanese inspired, but the artist was local. The two main characters were male best friends who refused to admit they were in love. She had a stunning grasp of the male form, and the way she alluded to their will-we-won't-we physical relationship was almost hotter than seeing it in vivid detail.

Almost. My imagination was happy to fill in the blanks. The same way it was doing right now with Fred and Barney. Hell, they could be the stars of the comic. Or my life. I didn't have any issue slotting them into a fantasy or two, where I was the middle in a Bedrock sandwich.

"No spoilers. I'm two books behind," Barney said.

He was reading this? "Then you probably don't want to know that Haru turns into a dragon halfway through this one, to save everyone from the Nazi invasion." I kept my tone serious. The series was strictly contemporary, with no magic, so I half-hoped he'd know I was teasing.

His grin was worth the joke. "I'd better catch up, then. Especially if there's a little bit of dragon-on-best-friend action."

"That's a disturbing image." Disturbingly intriguing.

Barney winked. "But you're totally trying to figure out the logistics anyway."

"Busted." I was enjoying this more than I'd expected.

Fred nudged his friend. "We'll let you get back to it. Thanks for letting us intrude."

I'd read a while longer, and if they got too loud I'd go. Right. Like I could focus with two mister hotties sitting right here.

They kept their voices low enough that I had to strain to hear them, even though they were only a few feet away. Sounded like they were from out of town, but loving the city, and hoping to see more of it while they were here.

I wasn't reading anything, despite trying my best to look like I was. I tried to block them out and pretend they weren't impacting my universe with their manga-come-to-life looks and politely low conversation. It didn't matter how hard I stared at the page in front of me, I wasn't processing any of the words.

A tickle bubbled in my throat, and I reached for my coffee. When my fingers collided with the cup instead of grasping it, my gut sank. I'd missed.

Iced coffee splashed everywhere. Down my shirt. Over my slacks. On their shoes.

"I'm so sorry." All my composure vanished, and I fumbled for napkins to mop the table.

Fred plucked my purse from the floor before the creeping puddle reached it, and my panic surged harder until he set the bag on my now-empty seat.

"Excuse me," Barney hollered at a nearby employee, cranking my humiliation higher. "Can we get a mop over here?" He left, and returned a moment later with a stack of napkins. He handed me several. "Take care of yourself. We've got this."

"Thank you," I mumbled, and started patting coffee from my once-white top. The liquid suctioned my clothes to me, clinging to my boobs, every fat roll. The sooner I got out of here, the sooner I could tumble backwards into humiliation. Until then, I was going to be collected.

I looked up to find Barney staring at me.

"Enjoying the show?" I hid a wince at the aggravation that slid into my voice.

He looked up, meeting my gaze unflinchingly. "Quite a bit." There was a sincerity and heat in his reply that scorched my already hot skin.

"Sorry about him." Fred elbowed Barney. "His filters don't always work right."

Barney didn't look fazed. "She asked, I gave her an honest answer."

"While she's all sticky and covered in coffee." Fred started undoing the buttons on his shirt. "Take this."

I held up a hand to stop him. Not that I would have minded the show. "I'm okay, really." I didn't look cute in a guy's shirt, the way some girls did. It would probably fit, but I wouldn't drown adorably in it. "Besides, we can't both be showing off our assets. People will get the wrong idea about this place."

"Do they have coffee shops like that? They should," Barney said.

If they were going to pretend this was no big deal, I could summon some phony self-assurance. Sex, fake confidence, and self-effacing humor had been my shield most of my life. "The kind where they spill your coffee on you instead of letting you drink it?

Barney looked me over again. Every time he did that, I swear I felt his gaze. "Assuming *they* is *you*, do I get to lick it off after?" he asked.

Was he hitting on me or making fun of me? It didn't matter. The coffee was drying and my clothes were getting uncomfortable. "I'm sorry about your shoes. Thanks for your help, but I need to get home."

I turned away, eager to escape the embarrassment and confusion.

Chapter Two

I was halfway to my car, when I heard, "Betty." Fred jogged up next to me. "Wow, that really does sound weak."

"It really does." I looked at him with raised brows, it probably wouldn't if it were my name, but it didn't escape me he still didn't offer his real name.

Barney joined us. "If you get in your car now, it gets covered in coffee too, and you have an uncomfortable drive home. We're staying next door. Walk over with us, and you can clean up in my room. Borrow something dry. Be on your way."

"Wow, that's…" I had no words.

"Super generous, right?" Barney winked. His *cute* was becoming *creepy*.

Fortunately, it helped me grab an answer. "A unique, but not super convincing way to get me to come back to your room."

Fred shrugged. "You're the one who spilled the coffee."

I didn't appreciate the reminder, but he said it without accusation or cruelty. He almost looked hurt at my tone. That hardly seemed fair. "Then this *isn't* a ploy to get me to join him in his room?" I asked.

"His room, my room. It absolutely is." Barney grinned.

It should have occurred to me to wonder before now, which of them was hitting on me? I'd say Barney, but Fred was working awfully hard to keep me happy. He was either one hell of a wingman, or...

No. There was no way it was both of them. Because that was what I'd been fantasizing about, and getting it would either be too much of a coincidence, or a cruelty when it went badly.

"But more people than you think tend to balk at the idea of two men from out of town trying to pick them up at the same time." There was a trace of humor in Barney's voice.

I pinched myself. Ow. Nope. I was still here. I did it again. Still hurt. Still didn't change the sexy dual scenery.

"What are you doing?" Barney asked.

"Trying to figure out what kind of dream this is." *Are you a good dream, or a bad dream*? The voice in my head sounded like the good witch from the Wizard of Oz. Maybe I'd dream of yellow brick roads next.

They chuckled, and Barney's smirk melted to something less cocky. "Since you don't seem interested, I'm making a genuine offer to let you clean up, which will be followed by a genuine offer to buy you a fresh cup of coffee after. And then we'll try again to seduce you."

"That sounds like a lot of trouble to go through for the woman who just spilled coffee all over herself." My brain wanted to say *chubby girl*, but I'd let the insult gnaw at me from the inside, rather than exposing it to them. "You could have let me walk away and found someone—" cuter, thinner, and less abrasive "—else to win over."

"If we'd been interested in someone else, we would have approached them instead." Did Fred sound… wounded?

A guy like this—like them—could smile at any other woman and have her. If he was hurt that I wasn't falling for the charm, he may be more concerned with hearing *no* or *yes* than who it came from. But he hadn't struck me that way up to this point. If I'd gone to the bar instead of the bookstore, I probably would have accepted their offer. I'd have been there for a hook-up, and they seemed sincere enough.

Except for the fake names.

They were cute. They were flirty. I did hate being covered in coffee.

And if it was so easy to lie to me about who they were, they were hiding other things as well. "I appreciate the offer, but I'm going to call it a night, gentlemen. I hope the hotel elephant shower has hot water, and that the stone houses aren't too drafty when you get back to Bedrock."

Barney laughed.

Fred gave me a short bow. "Yabba dabba doo, Betty. Maybe we'll run into you again before we leave town."

"Maybe." Unlikely. I'd probably avoid this bookstore for the next couple of weeks, specifically to keep that from happening. I was socially awkward that way.

There was a whisper of regret in my mind telling me stories of what could have been as I drove toward home. I couldn't help but replay the conversation in my mind. I was used to pick-up lines that reached *hey baby, let's fuck* without much hesitation. *Fred* and *Barney* actually made an effort. Plus, they were hitting on me *together*.

I'd made the right decision walking away, but everything about their attention painted a little smile on my face that didn't want to leave. Their company was fun while it lasted, and it had been a while since I walked away from two attractive maybe-hookups, and felt good about myself.

I parked around the back of my house. My café was up front, and took up the entire ground floor of the converted Victorian home. The rear stairs led up to the bedrooms and living area on the second floor.

asking for it

I'd gotten the house for an amazing price in auction. Low enough I could pay cash, and still have a little—very little—left over for renovations.

Until about a year ago, I'd always operated in the black. But I took a risk based on how well business was going, and secured a large loan to upgrade a lot of my equipment. Renovations slowed business enough both during and after, that I was struggling to pay that new bill.

There was an envelope slipped through the mail slot when I stepped inside. As I skimmed the formal notification on city letterhead, my heart sank.

A request for a zoning change had been filed, to remove residential properties from my area.

I'd had to fight to get my housing here to begin with. I couldn't afford to move to a new place now.

———

The sun was shining, the birds were singing, and okay, it sounded cliché, but I felt great in the morning. Sleep gave me enough sanity to know I could deal with the zoning issue just fine when the hearing happened in six weeks, and I still had warm fuzzies from the attention I got from Fred and Barney last night. I didn't mind blocking out the doubt, since it was a snapshot in time.

I put on one of my more fitted tops. It was sunny yellow, to match my mood, it did great things for my cleavage, and it mostly hid my tummy. I'd be standing to bake a lot of today, and wearing an apron, so I didn't have to worry about the space between the buttons gapping apart when I sat.

Living above my shop made for a convenient commute. In under a minute, I was in my gorgeous, big, industrial kitchen. Stainless steel appliances lined the walls, including three double-sized ovens opposite a massive fridge. In the middle stood a large island—half stainless steel, half butcher block. I loved this place, even if it was part of the reason I was struggling to make ends meet.

Today it would help pay for itself. I'd started taking on catering jobs to supplement the café's income. Tomorrow would be my biggest event yet. One hundred each cupcakes, bagels, croissants, and chocolate chip cookies, for the Digital Media company town hall.

Anne had teased me about working for the enemy—she was a game Director for DM's biggest competitor, Rinslet. But she's also told me if I happened to overhear any corporate secrets, she was happy to be my confidant.

She'd been joking. Mostly.

I set a pot of coffee to brew, and prepped my workspace for the pastries I needed to make for the shop this morning. Two hours later, I was on my third cup of coffee, and was setting the day's sweets under glass in the café.

Violet, my store manager, would be in soon to open up.

Time to get down to the big order. In my dreams, I was making enough money to hire more bakers. People I trusted as much as I did Violet to do their jobs without constant supervision. For now, the task of baking was mine.

I had a rhythm to my work that let me manage multiple batches at once. There was always a temptation to sample the goods, especially with me having skipped breakfast, but more coffee kept my stomach from growling.

The familiar ringtone that Anne, Sadie, and I all used for each other reached my ears. I pulled the call up on the tablet I kept on my counter, to find Anne grinning at me.

"You're baking," Anne said as a greeting.

I grinned. "What gave it away—the apron or the kitchen?" The happy note from last night still lingered in my thoughts. I turned back to my work, knowing she wouldn't mind.

"I'm just perceptive like that." Her tone was as bright and sunny as the weather. She'd had a long run of stress at work, but since a few things fell into place, she was a lot more like her old self. It was nice to hear. "Real quick, so you can work, girls' night out this weekend?"

Just the three of us? "Totally up for that."

"Yay. So, what has you humming?"

Was I? "I'll share details, but not until we're face-to-face. This weekend, probably."

"I'm never going to live that down, am I?" Anne laughed. When she'd first hooked up with her guys—as in her boss and Sadie's brother—she put off telling us by saying she'd rather have the conversation face-to-face.

"Maybe someday. Just not today." I turned to find her pouting at the camera. Too adorable. "All right, I'll spill. Otherwise you'll think it's a big deal, and it's not. I got hit on last night, and while it didn't go anywhere, it made me feel good."

"You're being vague with your pronouns."

No. Just with my counting. "Because it's not a big deal, because it didn't go anywhere. Text me details for this weekend."

As I resumed working, I tried out the humming again. I liked that. I kept a tuneless song flitting around me as I worked on cupcakes. Those needed to bake and cool first, so I could decorate them while everything else was cooking.

It might have been nice to lose track of time, but with a timer on each step, that wasn't happening. Still, the next couple of hours passed quickly.

"There's someone here to see you." Violet's cheerful voice startled me as I was stepping away from the oven.

Not the best timing, but not the worst either. "Do me a favor, keep an eye on those." I nodded to the oven. "If I'm not back in twenty-five minutes, take them out?"

"No problem."

I dusted the flour from my apron before hanging it up on its hook, and headed out into the main shop.

Fred and *Barney* were standing near the front counter. They were dressed differently than last night, both looking gorgeously sexy in suits that accentuated their sturdy builds, ties that my imagination wanted used on me, and flat expressions that growled *don't fuck with us.*

My stomach turned in on itself, and every muscle in my body tensed. How did they find me? Did they follow me home?

Chapter Three

I'd pushed my luck for far too long, making a habit of one-night stands with strangers I met in bars. And now the one time I'd picked a bookstore instead, I'd managed to run into not one, but two creepy stalkers. If I screamed, Violet would call the police. The thought didn't reassure me the way I wanted it to.

"What are you doing here?" I kept my tone steady, despite my creeping fear. "Did you follow me home last night?"

Fred frowned. He had the nerve to look offended? Now? Or was that his normal look? "I'm looking for Jaelyn O'Driscoll. Are you she?"

How the fuck did he know not only my name, but all of it? "May I tell her who's asking?"

"Owen Samson." He extended his hand, and nodded at Barney. My already churning gut plummeted into my feet, and I knew he was going to say, "and my associate Kingston Ryder."

Fuck. Fear bled into irritation. These were the two assholes who had been trying to buy out my business for several months. And last night I'd considered going back to their hotel? Worse, I'd enjoyed their company.

I crossed my arms rather than shake his hand. "I'm still not interested. Now that we've covered that, I have a huge catering order I need to get back to. I trust you can find your way out as easily as you found your way in."

"Sharp wit *and* dangerous curves. You're destruction in a stunning package." Kingston used the same flirty tone he had as Barney.

Why was a sliver of me still enjoying him? Still sending shivers of desire through me while my brain begged me to indulge a fantasy. "If I'd realized last night that you're the kind of men who can't take *no* for an answer—"

"We have a new offer for you, and it's a good one," Owen said.

I clenched my jaw at being cut off. If I screamed, I'd look irrational and unreasonable, even though they were the ones who kept coming back after I turned them away. It was tempting to scream.

Kingston's smirk didn't improve my mood. "Not as good an offer as last night."

And now he was mixing business with pleasure? Implying screwing him was better than… whatever this was?

Then again, this was irritating the hell out of me, so sex probably would be better.

Bad libido. Stop.

Owen sighed. "Don't listen to him, he forgot to put his dick away. We're here on business. Nothing else."

"Something we agree on." I gave them a thin smile. "This is absolutely nothing, because you're leaving."

"Five minutes." Kingston's tone and posture changed like a switch had been flipped. His playfulness disappeared behind an intimidating mask of seriousness.

This was why I hadn't recognized their voices last night. Kingston was always the one to call me, to negotiate, and this voice was different than the flirty, carefree one he'd approached me with in the bookstore.

I could reinforce a third time that they needed to leave. But if I heard them out, and their offer sucked as much as I expected it to, I'd have blocked off more of their avenues for arguing. I hated knowing they could control the conversation this way, but I was going to close every loophole they could find, until they heard me. "Five minutes. I won't start a timer, but make it fast, and make it good."

asking for it

I shouldn't have phrased it that way. *We always take our time, and it's* always *good.* I swore I could hear Kingston's voice in my head.

His lips twitched, and I pursed my lips, daring him to take the accidental innuendo outlet.

Owen elbowed him, and his serious mask was back in place.

"May we do this in your office?" Owen asked.

No, because my body was still reacting to them. It didn't matter that it shouldn't be. We'd stay in a public place, where it was easier to remind myself that everything about them right now was pissing me off.

Even admit the memories of how nice last night was. How they'd looked at me. How sincere and complimentary they were… "Out here is fine. Did you know who I was yesterday?"

"No," Kingston said quickly. "The only Jaelyn we know is the curvy avatar."

Call me Lyn. I swallowed the offer. Only my friends called me Lyn.

He was talking about the woman in my shop's logo. The cute one with the generous hips and breasts, and a waist I'd never have. She looked like me as much as she looked like any voluptuous brunette. I went out of my way to keep my own face off social media—I hated pictures of myself. I didn't even let Sadie post me on her different pages.

But Owen and Kingston were the same. I'd dug into them a lot in the past year. They identified their company with names and a logo. I'd never been able to find a single picture of either of them. I'd assumed they were rich old assholes who didn't understand social media.

Turns out they were rich younger assholes, who probably understood more than they let people know.

"What's this proposal and why is it so much better than the previous ones?" I asked.

Owen pulled an index card from his jacket pocket. "Ten percent over the previous amount." He needed notes to tell him that?

"Wow. That's *so* much better." I let the sarcasm spill into my retort. "Answer's still *no*. Wow, that didn't even take one minute. Have a nice da—"

"There's more," Kingston said smoothly. "And fuck, you make it hard. To behave."

I was getting real sick of them talking over me, especially since that pause in his phrasing was intentional. I was as mad at the part of me loving the flirting as I was at them. It would be so easy to slide into a playful comeback. A lot more difficult to forget who they were, in order to do so. "You were saying?"

Kingston's smirk was back. Sexy, arrogant jerk. "Most of the cafes we bring on are happy to take our money and step aside. We made a mistake assuming that was what you'd want to do as well."

Thank you, Captain Obvious. I swallowed my retort. The sooner they finished their spiel, the sooner I could get rid of them.

"You built the place, you love the place, I get that." Kingston sounded sincere. He was good at faking it, apparently. "I understand that more than you might believe."

"That's not a high bar." I couldn't help myself.

The corners of Owen's mouth twitched. "You keep the property. The new amount is only for the business. We'll rent the shop space from you, ask you to keep running the place, and double your salary. The only thing that really changes is we acquire your business's debt, you'll have access to our suppliers, and we'll put our sign in the window next to yours. This remains *Loading Java*, it simply comes a subsidiary of Kingu Kafes."

It was an implausibly sweet deal. On the surface. It was tempting to say *I'm in*. It would solve the letter from last night. It would solve a lot of things. It was also too good to be true. I had questions—the same ones they'd never answered in the past. For instance, how were they going to afford to be so generous, when I could barely keep the place operating the black?

"For that kind of money, you could set up your own shop. Why are you so focused on mine?"

"You have a customer base, a solid brand, and reliable product," Kingston said. "Competing with you thins the local market as well as our chances of succeeding."

That made sense. "And your solution is give me a lot of money, and beyond that, everything is business as usual." It wasn't quite that cut-and dried though.

Kingston nodded.

Owen looked more hesitant.

"Until you decide you don't like how I do things, and you override me by either firing me or buying me out." With as starkly as we clashed now, I didn't suspect that would take long.

Owen furrowed his brow. "We don't plan on—"

"My answer is still *no*." It felt good to be the one talking over him. "I run my café the way I do, because I like having this control. This is my business. My investment. My passion. Thank you for your time. See your way ou—"

The loud blare of the fire alarm cut me off, shrieking so sharply it threatened to pierce my eardrums.

Chapter Four

Smoke. Now that I wasn't distracted, the heavy smell hit me hard. I rushed to the kitchen. My only priority was finding the source and shutting it down.

Violet was already at the oven, muttering and pulling out smoldering trays of cupcakes. The panic in her expression grew when she saw me. "I'm so sorry. I had a customer, they kept me longer than I realized. I'm so sorry." Red splotched her cheeks and deep creases marred her forehead.

She was typically too detailed and aware to let things like this happen. The freaking out she was doing right now was rare.

"It happens. It's okay." I was stressed too, but I didn't blame her. "I need you to shut off the fire alarm. Call the fire department and let them know there's nothing wrong. Clear people out of the shop and open all the doors." As I talked, I ticked off the list in my mind. Lists made me calmer. "Anyone currently here gets a $5 gift card for their next visit. Put a sign on the counter that gives everyone 5% off pastries for the rest of the day, as an apology for the smoke smell. Do you have all that?"

Violet nodded.

I knew she would. She was my store manager for a reason. "You all right?" I softened my tone. "This isn't a big deal. No one got hurt. Everything will be all right."

"Okay." Her smile was weak, not hiding the lingering stress. She headed toward the alarm shut off.

As soon as she left the room, I sank against a nearby counter and let the panic overwhelm me. I'd already had a long day with baking and everything else. This would only add another hour or so onto the end of my day, if everything went perfectly, but I was going to be exhausted by the end of the original schedule.

Emotion indulged, I breathed in and out slowly several times to force it away. I turned to grab my apron.

When I saw Owen and Kingston near the kitchen doorway, I jumped in surprise, and my heart lodged in my throat. Why did they follow me?

I didn't have the time or patience for this. I tugged on my apron, never making eye contact with them. They'd seen me crack, but they wouldn't see me break. "Something I can help you with, that we haven't already discussed to death?"

asking for it

"Actually, we'd like to help you." Owen was calm. Smooth.

No, really. I had zero time. "Are you going to magic a hundred chocolate and vanilla cupcakes out of thin air."

Kingston smirked. "Sort of."

I was learning to love-loathe his sexy, smug face. Was that a thing? I was making it a thing.

"I did two years at a Cordon Bleu school in Massachusetts. You tell me what you need done, and I'll do it," Owen said.

Of course he had. Mister sexy, rich businessman was also a baker. I'd read it on his profile on his company's site, but I figured it was just words to give their investments in cafes some credibility. I looked at Kingston, waiting for a similar boast. "And you?"

He shrugged. "I did two years of being a short order cook. I can follow instructions like no one's business."

"Why would you help me?" I didn't understand.

"Because you're sexy and stressed." Kingston's flirting didn't seem to be just for show. He slid into it without hesitation.

I shot a glare at him. "Try again."

Owen had probably been the straight man for as long as they'd known each other. "Because you're catering under a label we're trying to purchase, and at the end of the day, we'd rather its reputation stay solid."

That actually made sense. "This isn't going to change my mind."

"Didn't think it would. Clock is ticking?"

And I loathe-loved Owen's gorgeous perfect way of looking good and being rational and saying all the right things at the wrong time.

I pointed. "Aprons are behind you, sink is behind me. Wash up. You're going to get your suits dirty. And you realize I'm just using you for the manual labor."

"Worth it." Owen had already pulled off his suit coat and hung it out of the way. He rolled his shirt sleeves up, exposing an intricate Celtic knot tattoo trailing up the inside of his arm.

I'd never been an arm girl before, but strength and surety in his movement made me want to whimper in delight. I turned away before I could imagine him pinning me to the wall by my wrists and running his lips over—

Nope. I was on a deadline, and he was one of the assholes trying to buy my dream out from underneath me.

They'd offered to help, and if they were competent, I was going to take it. "The bad cupcakes need to be thrown out, and the pans cleaned."

asking for it

Kingston grabbed the first muffin tin. "Master dishwasher at your service."

I wasn't going to let them do anything that could slow me down more, but with the extra I'd made of certain items, that still left me with a list of tasks. "There's dough for croissants in the walk-in, in big plastic containers. Start kneading a batch." Might as well get Owen moving on those, since they'd take the next most time. See if he was worth what he said.

"You got it, boss." He vanished into the fridge, and reemerged with one of the tubs of dough.

We worked for the next couple of hours. They picked up every task I gave them without complaint, and by the time afternoon rolled around, I was ahead of schedule rather than behind.

I'd be out of here long before midnight, the scenery was stunning when it was quiet… My day was looking up after all.

"Who delivers the best food around here?" Kingston's question was the first non-baking one anyone had asked since we dove into work.

I needed more information to respond, though. "Pretty much anything is available on one of the apps."

"I'll rephrase that. We need to eat, what do you recommend?"

That they not watch me eat. My schedule didn't allow for meal breaks on days like this, but I wasn't up for stuffing my face in front of them anyway. "Depends on what you're in the mood for."

Owen paused in his bagel shaping duties, and held my gaze with a penetrating stare. "What do *you* want? You can't say *nothing*."

"Why not?" Maybe they hadn't caught on yet, I didn't respond well to being told what I couldn't do.

"Because you're swaying on your feet. You can't run on coffee alone."

I could and I had. But arguing with them would make this into a big deal, and I didn't want that. "There's a great Chinese place just a couple of blocks away. They have fantastic pork soup dumplings." The owner was as white as anyone, but he'd gone to Hong Kong on a Mormon mission, decided he liked cooking more than the faith he'd been raised in, was trained by a local master, and came back to open his own restaurant.

"That sounds great." Kingston pulled out his phone.

"Menu and phone number are in the binder on the counter." I pointed. "I'll have the side salad with ginger dressing." The twin looks of disbelief I received were almost accusatory. "I'm not that hungry."

My bitch of a stomach chose that moment to growl and betray me.

Owen raised an eyebrow. "I'll have what she recommended."

Kingston called in the order, which included three helpings of soup dumplings, plus my salad. Either I did a fantastic job upselling the food, or he was assuming and ordering for me. I wasn't going to make a fuss out of it. If one of them was going to eat it, fine. If they tried to give it to me, that was their mistake.

We worked until the food came, then set up a space away from the work area, with three stools pulled up to an island.

Sure enough, Kingston slid me a bowl of pork dumplings, along with my salad.

I pushed the extra food back. "This isn't what I ordered."

"But it's what you wanted," Owen said.

He was right, but I didn't appreciate the assumption. Just like that, a morning of peace evaporated, and my irritation was back. Half at them, for going against my wishes, and half at myself for being too stubborn to take the food.

Chapter Five

Kingston nudged the dumplings back toward me. "If you keep eating rabbit food, you'll damage those curves."

I clenched my jaw. Jokes about my weight were at the top of my *things I hate* list. Go figure. But that wasn't what he'd done.

He was watching me with a *look* again—one that set my blood on fire. The food *did* smell good, but I didn't like that they'd ordered for me when I told them not to. "I'm good with the salad. Now you have leftovers for later."

"No fridges in our hotel rooms," Owen said. "The food stays with you unless you want it to go to waste."

They were backing me into a corner, the way they kept trying to do with buy-out negotiations. And I wasn't making a big deal out of this. I moved the box to sit outside my arm. I'd have Violet take it home or something. "Fine."

I plucked cucumber slice from my salad and nibbled it far longer than I needed to. The dumplings looked good and smelled better. Why did they have to force my hand?

Kingston wielded his chopsticks with ease as he took a bite of food. His groan was a low, throaty rumble that sent pleasant shivers racing over me.

Own was using a spoon, and his moan was just as tempting. "You're right. This is incredible."

Jerks. They were doing that on purpose.

"I know you're not hungry"—Kingston sectioned off another bit on chopsticks—"but you have room for one bite." He held the food out.

I could eat that and be delicate, and then we could drop the entire conversation. I leaned in and took the food offering. As I licked my lips, I earned another groan. I was going to bake under the intense heat of Kingston's gaze.

I must have been bright red as I turned back to my salad. It didn't look as appetizing now that I had the other flavors on my tongue, but this was about pride and proving a point.

"Would you like another bite?" Owen teased his fork near me.

This was just mean. "I'm fine."

"You look a bit put out."

"But you still look *fine*," Kingston said. "I'll agree with that."

The flirting was going to get old. It hadn't yet, but I was sure it would. "I'm not that girl."

"What girl?" Owen put his spoon down.

"The one who says she doesn't want anything, and then eats half her—" I couldn't say *date* or *boyfriend* "—dining companion's food. Besides, I have my own, which was thoughtful, if not presumptuous, of you."

"Fuck, you're stubborn." Kingston sounded amused.

"Says the man who refuses to take *no* for an answer."

"If you want the food, eat the food. It's not like you care what we think," Owen said.

"And *you're* infuriatingly logical."

Kingston laughed. "Isn't he, though? That's why he lets me do the negotiating. People want to come to the bargaining table with their hearts, not their minds, regardless of what they say. You, for instance, are looking at our offer mostly based on your heart."

"I told you this was my passion. You don't need a psychology degree to figure out I'm not turning you away because of the money." I didn't care for being analyzed, even if I was doing the same to them. But Owen had a point, too. If I didn't care what they thought of me, why was I hesitating to eat? And now I'd done the one thing I didn't want to—made a big deal out of the food.

"I'm not doing this because you're right. About anything." I set my salad aside, grabbed a pair of chopsticks, and plucked a dumpling from the broth.

"Of course you're not." Owen kept a straight face.

Kingston was smirking though.

It was a good thing they were leaving at the end of the day. They wreaked havoc on my mind and body, and part of me wanted a lot more of the same.

I really wanted the focus off me and my dietary choices. Always, but especially now. "How long are you two going to be in town?" That was polite and gave me information at the same time. It would tell me how long I needed to hide and avoid them.

The glances they exchanged were impossible to interpret.

"Is it a secret?" I asked.

Owen opened his mouth.

"Yes." Kingston talked over him. "At least for now it is."

"Ah." Not that it was really my business, but it was an odd thing to not want to discuss. "Then, how about that gorgeous weather we're having? Or are your thoughts on that a secret too?" I kept my tone light.

"It *was* a secret, but then the press caught wind, and social media started talking, and now *everyone* knows I think the weather is perfect right now."

Kingston finished with an exaggerated sigh, and the corners of his eyes still crinkled with laughter.

If he weren't gorgeous and rich and completely on top of the world, I might start to think the steady stream of humor was there to mask an insecurity.

"Speaking of the gorgeous weather—" Owen looked like a light bulb had just gone off in his mind —"we're meeting a few friends up at Strawberry Reservoir on Sunday. They've got a huge cabin up there. You should come with us."

Besides the fact that the invitation was completely out of the blue, the lake meant water meant boats and swimming and most likely people in bathing suits. Not for me. "Why?"

"They come from some of the more influential families around here," Owen said. "In politics. In money. It's a good chance to make some connections."

"Also, they're fun. Otherwise, what's the point?" Kingston added.

That still didn't answer my question. "I'll be clearer. Why *me*?"

"You're smart. You're an excellent businesswoman." Owen ticked off bullet points.

I stared at him blankly. "Which doesn't translate to *come hang at the lake with us and meet our rich friends*. You barely know me."

asking for it

Owen raised an eyebrow. "We're still trying to make you a business partner, and this is a good excuse to get to know you in a social-but-professional environment."

And there it was. His answer didn't bother me the way I thought it should.

"Some people think it doesn't matter who you know, but it does. Use this to your advantage," Kingston said.

I hated the idea of owing anyone or calling in favors, but Kingston was right. Their reasons for introducing me didn't have to be mine. "Don't suppose any of your friends are connected to the city council." As in, could they put me in touch with someone who could help me with my zoning issues?

Not that I'd skirt the system that way, but I'd feel a little better about my upcoming hearing if I knew someone.

"As a matter of fact, yes," Owen said.

"Sounds like fun." I was making a mistake, accepting. But they were here on business, and had made no illusions about it. I doubted they had any false ideas about why I'd join them anywhere else, either.

The conversation drifted back to barely-there small talk. We finished lunch, and dove back into baking.

"The limited edition poster you have for X-10, in the café." Owen shaped out bagels like a pro. "We called in every favor we could think of, and couldn't get one of those. How'd you manage it?"

Kingston rolled his eyes. "He's a fanboy. Don't get him started, or he'll never stop."

"What did you think of how it ended?" My question was leading. A lot of the *fanboys* had a problem with the way the X franchise had wrapped up. In the final game, the hero confessed his love to the man he'd been sent to execute in Game 1, but whom he saved instead.

If Owen fell into that category, maybe it would be enough to tell my libido to calm the heck down and stop drooling over him.

"Loved it." Owen's excitement shone in his gaze. It was the most emotion I'd seen from him. "That ninth game shook my faith, but 10... *Wow*. I should have seen it coming, and I didn't. Brilliant. Appropriate. Possibly my favorite game ever."

I'd pass the praise along to Anne, but why couldn't he have been an ass about the whole thing? "It is pretty good."

"And the poster?" Owen asked.

I shrugged. "I fucked one of the developers."

Kingston looked impressed. "I hope he was worth a poster."

asking for it

"*She* is worth a lot more than that. But we make better friends than lovers." Why had I gone out of my way to bring up what Anne and I used to have? To prove to them I was desirable, or to remind myself?

Neither of them looked fazed. Bonus points to them for not casting judgement, though a hint of jealousy might have been nice.

"So, is X's relationship based on you two?" Owen's question was light and playful.

Anne wasn't involved in the writing, just the programming. "Well, she did pretend to execute me once, in order to save my life. Slid her cart racer into mine, to push me out of the way of a blue turtle shell. But we didn't swear vengeance on the legions who did it."

"No?" Kingston leaned against a nearby counter, palms rested on the butcher block top. "Because that's some pretty serious shit."

"Everyone gets a little power hungry when they're playing a mushroom driving a cartoon car. He lost anyway, so I suppose fate stepped in on our behalf."

Chase could be a sabotaging asshole in Mario Kart, but Anne loved him and he was Sadie's brother, so we forgave him the competitive streak.

"So are you a Princess Peach kind of player? Toad?" Owen asked.

"Donkey Kong."

Owen's eyes grew wide. "You know how to control that slide?"

"Better than anyone, especially if they try to pass me in the corners."

"Brutal." Kingston sounded appreciative. "That's sexy."

I flushed at his sincerity. Not used to not having a comeback, I turned my attention back to making buttercream frosting.

The only way I had to measure time was by how much we got done. I was still surprised when Violet poked her head in.

"Store's locked up," she said. "Do you need anything"—she glanced at the men—"or do you want me to stick around at all?" Her implied meaning *are you all right alone with two strange guys* was clear.

I gave her a reassuring smile. "I'll be okay, thank you. Enjoy your night."

She gave me one last wave, and was gone.

Owen offered to help decorate the cupcakes. That was a little more control than I wanted to give up, but I also wanted to finish. I made him prove himself by piping on a piece of wax paper, and was impressed with the results.

We worked for a couple more hours, putting the finishing touches on everything, and boxing it all up.

asking for it

"Last one." Owen added the box of cupcakes to the stack, and turned to face me.

He had two almost perfect smudges of chocolate on his forehead, that made him look like he had double eyebrows and was very surprised. I bit my lip to hide my amusement, but a laugh slipped out.

"What did I miss?" He raised an eyebrow. That made it even funnier.

Kingston joined in the laughing. "Chocolate on your face."

"Where?" Owen frowned.

I shouldn't keep laughing, but I couldn't help it. "Your forehead. Here." I crossed the distance between us, and smudged the frosting away with a towel.

"You think that's funny?" Owen's tone was threatening, but he was smiling too.

"A little, yeah."

He booped my nose. "There. Now you have chocolate on your face too."

"You jerk." I reached to wipe it away.

Owen grabbed my wrist. "Leave it. It looks cute."

A shiver of desire ran through me at the heat of his grip, and when I met his gaze, my breath caught at the intensity staring back.

Now would be the perfect time to pull away. But my body was too focused on the heat flowing between us and the faint scent of his cologne mixed with sugar, to get the message.

Chapter Six

I forced myself to act, dipping a free finger in the extra frosting, and aiming a touch for Owen's cheek.

He captured my other wrist as well. His grip was more solid and tantalizing than my fantasies promised, and now my brain was skipping ahead to the part where he'd pin me to the wall—

"What are you going to do now?" Owen's tone was teasing mixed with challenge.

Whimper and beg him to lift me on the counter and take advantage of me? "Pout?" I jutted out my lower lip.

Kingston had gone quiet. Was he watching? Enjoying or irritated?

"That's not a deterrent." Owen pulled my frosting covered finger into his mouth.

When he traced circles over my skin, licking it clean, that whimper escaped.

His smirk was another layer of delicious. He dropped that wrist, still studying me. "Next plan?" He asked.

I nodded at my still captured hand. "You got chocolate on my wrist, too." I'd stop short of asking him to lick every inch of me—probably.

A touch met the small of my back. "Save some for me." There was Kingston. He grasped my fingertips.

Owen let me go to reach past me and grip the back of Kingston's neck. He crushed his mouth to Kingston's in the sort of all-consuming kiss that made my lips whimper for a hint of the same.

I think my gasp was as loud as Kingston's when they broke apart.

Kingston chuckled softly and bit his bottom lip. "I meant the gorgeous lady's chocolate frosting, but that's pretty good too."

Just. Wow.

The way they interacted with me, with each other, told me they were practiced at this two-guys-one-girl thing. Not that I expected to be their first. I was here for the physical gratification. The show between the two of them was an added bonus. Were they more than friends? They must be with a kiss like that.

When Kingston licked the sensitive skin along the inside of my wrist, my questions faded into the background and I moaned. That felt better than should be legal.

asking for it

"Good?" he asked with a grin. His composure had returned.

Mine hadn't. Any answer I could come up with felt weak, so I settled for nodding.

He increased the pressure of his tongue, alternating between licking and sucking, until goosebumps raised over every inch of me, and my nipples strained against my bra, wanting to feel this for themselves.

"Did you plan this?" My doubt was a bitch for trying to ruin this moment.

Owen twisted his mouth. "Which one of us?"

"You seem to work together pretty well, so both or either?"

Owen dipped his finger in the frosting again, and trailed a line down the side of my neck. He leaned in and dragged his tongue up the same curve, stopping with his lips on my earlobe. "Did we plan for you to burn dozens of cupcakes?" he whispered. "To have a deadline. To be willing to accept our help. To be so much fun to talk to, on top of being sexy as fuck?"

When he put it that way…

He caught my earlobe between his teeth, and tugged before pulling away to look me in the eye. "No. But if I had, I couldn't have hoped for better."

"What if I kick you out right now, with a terse *thank you*, and that's that?" I wasn't going to do that.

They were delicious and there was nothing wrong with a physical, no-strings outlet to relieve stress, if that was where this was going. It didn't even matter that they were my rivals. It wasn't like I had to look them in the eye on a daily basis.

Kingston turned me toward him. "Then you kick us out. It was still a good day." Damn him for saying the right thing. "Are you telling us to leave?"

"No."

He was close enough I could see a faint dusting of flour in the dark stubble on his jaw. He fiddled with the top button on my blouse, tugging the fabric aside.

"Good. Because I can't help but wonder, what you'd look like in just this apron." He was making it difficult to remember why I didn't care to have them in my life. He scraped my skin with a fingernail, stealing my breath.

I took the apron off. Was that better, or worse? "You're not finding out today." I kept my tone playful.

"What if"— He trailed a finger along my chest, following the curve of my shirt, dipping into my cleavage —"I want to see what you look like with nothing on at all? I've been fantasizing about unwrapping you since last night." He dipped his head next to my ear, hot breath caressing my cheek. "If I drag my tongue over your bare skin, do you taste like salted caramel?"

Absolutely not. That was ridiculous. "Only one way to find out." My response came out breathy. My pulse hammered in my ears at my own challenge—this kitchen was public. A lot of people got off to the idea of getting caught, but it was one of my top fears. Was there a phobia based on that?

Focus. Two gorgeous men were showering me with compliments and kisses, this was my place, even if it was in the business part of the building, and no one else was here now.

Kingston undid one button and then another, until my blouse hung open.

And there was another surge of insecurity; in this brightly lit room, my less-than stunning body would be on display.

He tugged the fabric open, exposing bare skin and breasts straining against pale satin. The way he raked his gaze over me, I suddenly felt like a goddess.

"Fucking gorgeous." Kingston slid his hands up my sides and his lips down my neck. He kissed along my collarbone and down to the top of my breasts, teasing his thumbs over the cups.

Owen trailed his fingers lightly up my spine, almost enough to tickle, but the sensation was too tantalizing to pull away. He unclasped my bra with a deft twist. The tension that fell away was nothing compared to the anticipation that replaced it.

With double the attention, it was easy for me to fall into the physical. Owen kneading one breast while he nibbled on my neck and shoulder. Kingston drawing a nipple into his mouth to suck and lick.

The attention drew on, building the desire that raced over me and wrapping me up in the illusion of being wanted. Needed. I didn't care that they'd done this before with anyone else. It meant they knew where to touch to make me moan and squirm. Their touches were a delicate ballet of hands and mouths, and my body was the stage.

Kingston ran a hand down my back, over the curve of my ass, to my leg, and pulled my leg to his thigh. He slid a knee between my legs.

Without Owen there, chest and erection pressed into my side and hip, I wouldn't have the balance for this.

Kingston pressed his leg higher, against my mound, and I ground into him. A new point of contact drew another sigh from me. The way he groaned into my skin, still worshipping one nipple then the other with his mouth, cranked my need higher.

I had to feel more. As much as I could. *Everything*. I dragged my nails down Owen's chest, to his hard length. When I cupped him through his trousers, he jerked into my touch with a dangerously delicious moan. He was hard and thick, pressing into my palm as I stroked him.

Kingston let my leg down, and raised his head as he knotted his fingers in my hair. His dark eyes sparkled with promises of mischief.

I could drown in that look.

He brushed his mouth over mine. "Better than salted caramel." He nipped my bottom lip. "Better than anything salty or sweet." He tightened his grip in my hair, tugging hard enough to draw a gasp from me. "Better than anything." He kissed me hard.

My mind sang and whimpered and begged for more.

Kingston undid my slacks, and slid his hand under the waistband, over my panties, teasing me through fabric.

I gripped Owen tighter, and he bit my shoulder.

The sting of pleasure and pain was new to me, and incredible.

Kingston kissed along my jaw up to my opposite ear. "I fell asleep last night dreaming of fucking you. You were incredible then. You're better in real life." His whispered words, the flattery, were more effective than poetry.

"Do you have condoms?" I wasn't so far lost as to skip important steps, but I was getting close.

Kingston pulled back to meet my gaze again. He wore a dangerously hungry smirk as he extracted a condom from his wallet and held it up between two fingers like a prize.

In a disruption of hands, and my nervous giggle when my pants got stuck on my shoes, my clothes were shoved to the ground and kicked aside.

I unzipped Kingston's trousers, reveling in his throaty gasp when I wrapped my hand around his shaft. He bit his bottom lip, looking like it took immense effort to pull away and roll on the condom.

Kingston's hands on my hips, he guided me to a nearby stool, and nudged me to sit. I didn't like the absence of Owen's touch. I was greedy to have both of them embracing me again.

And then he was there again, half-supporting me, turning my head to face him so he could claim my lips.

Kingston slid between my legs, which parted eagerly, and dragged the head of his cock along my slit, teasing until I whimpered against Owen's kisses.

When Kingston pushed inside me, spreading me open and stretching me out, I let out a muffled gasp. He worked to a steady pace, thrusting enough to build my pleasure, and bring it to a heady ledge. He dropped his head to my breasts again, to suck on a nipple.

Owen worked a hand between us, down my stomach, to find my clit. He circled the swollen button, faster, harder.

Climax surged through me without warning, splashing around me. Consuming me. I clenched around Kingston, lost in orgasm, my body shuddering away when Owen's touch became too much.

More. The insistence was louder now, rather than being sated. I fumbled my way through unzipping Owen's slacks, and freed him. The noises they made, the attention they gave me, the scents of sugar and sex, were better than the finest liquor, going straight to my head.

Kingston increased the pace and intensity, slamming against me, inside me, striking the right spot and breathing new fire into a fading orgasm.

I stroked Owen in rhythm with the pump of Kingston's hips. Gripping tighter as another wave of pressure built inside me.

Owen covered my hand, setting the pace, not letting up even as I came again, tumbling into the sea of sparkles that danced behind my eyelids.

Twin grunts, staccato and wrapped in climaxes of their own, filtered into the haze I floated in. Fingers dug into my hips. Warm sticky fluid covered my hand.

The world slowly swam back into focus as we slowed and stopped. Owen was behind me, holding me upright, and Kingston had his forehead buried in the crook of my neck.

It would be a little while before I wanted to move from this spot. The impulse was there to cover up. At least grab the apron Kingston said he wanted to see me naked under.

But it was easy to ignore the thought, nestled between them.

"So…" Kingston kissed along my shoulder. "You'll take a look at the contract now?"

Ice raced through my veins, freezing my entire body.

Owen's groan was a different one than he'd been making all day. This sound was less sexy and more disbelief.

I forced myself to move. To extract myself from the pile of limbs, and grabbed the apron. It wasn't enough. I needed a dozen layers of clothing between me and them. "Get out." I bit off the words.

They were both already on their feet, straightening their clothes. Buttoning and zipping up.

"I didn't mean it like that," Kingston sounded apologetic.

Which was bullshit. At least I could recognize that now.

"Please." Owen studied me with… pity?

I didn't want his fucking pity.

"Let me explain—"

"Listen to me." I interrupted Kingston with bitten off words. "Don't talk. We're done. Get. *Out*." I spoke through gritted teeth. I refused to break in front of them, no matter how desperately I wanted to shatter into a million pieces.

Chapter Seven

The catering for Digital Media consumed enough of my brain that I could ignore yesterday, and what happened with Kingston and Owen. But as the event wound down and exhaustion sank into my bones, my brain was free to skip along any path it wanted.

By the time I got back to my apartment above the shop, my thoughts were berating me full-force.

I fell for the guys' bullshit, less than a day after they lied to me about who they were. It hurt from my toes to my hair follicles, that I'd let down my guard even a little. What was I thinking?

I was an idiot. Sex didn't equal a connection and neither did good conversation. A lot of people knew how to get along.

But this was different.

Was it? If I hadn't enjoyed their company, I wouldn't have screwed them. The day was fun, the sex was good, and I got to try the whole two-guys-at-once thing. Honestly, I'd expected disappointment, but that was good—*really* good—so I could check that off my non-existent bucket list.

It was sorted then. I'd had fun, no one used anyone, even though apparently that was what they'd been trying for, and it was time for me to move on. I hadn't been an idiot after all, just made a few naive assumptions.

My thoughts didn't get the memo, though. Through the night and into the next morning, I was treated to replays of Kingston's kisses and Owen's touches and two skilled lovers savoring me like the most delicious delicacy.

As I made pastries for the shop, ghosts teased me with memories of them both working in my kitchen. Of the synchronicity we'd achieved. Of how good they looked in aprons, with their sleeves rolled up.

This wasn't working for me. I didn't swoon over one-night stands. Especially when they turned out to be assholes.

That must be why I couldn't move on. I'd resigned myself to the fact that most guys I hooked up with were either desperate and horny, or looking to fulfill some fuck-a-fat-chick fantasy, though they rarely said so.

But Owen and Kingston did it to get at my shop, and they never tried to hide that fact. It made me feel like merchandise. The extra two dollars spent to get ten dollars in free shipping.

"Do you have a minute?" Violet startled me from my staring off into space.

I shook away the haze of thoughts, and caught sight of the clock. Shit, the pastries. "Yeah. What's up?" I rushed for the oven, and pulled out the Danishes with plenty of time left to prevent another yesterday. I needed to stop spacing out.

"So, Anne is like a big deal over at Rinslet, right?" Violet asked.

I turned to face her. "She'd tell you not really, but she is." I'd take any chance I could to brag about my friends' accomplishments.

Violet lingered in the doorway, tangling and untangling her fingers. "I've got this friend, Luna, who's an amazing programmer. She's seriously top notch. But she's having trouble breaking into... well... anything. Sorry, *breaking into* was a bad phrase. She can't get anyone to take her seriously. I was wondering if Anne could give her some tips?"

"I'll ask and let you know, but probably." The answer would be *yes*. Anne loved to help other women get a foothold in development, but it wasn't my place to speak for her.

Violet grinned. "Thank you. I'm gonna open shop."

asking for it

This was the life I'd built for myself—the life I wanted—with my café running smoothly, and friends who could count on me. I wouldn't let a pair of pushy—sexy, talented, intelligent, incredible in bed—strangers occupy space in my mind

While I worked, I called Anne on speakerphone. I wasn't in the mood to be on camera, even for her.

Her cheer when she answered made me smile a little, and the small talk helped more. I needed to get Owen and Kingston out of my head and telling her would help.

"Violet wants me to ask you a favor." I explained the same thing Violet had told me. Business first, and then I could expose a portion of my gullible soul.

"I'd love to help." Anne was cheerful. "Oh, idea. Would you be okay with them joining us Saturday night?"

"Of course." My answer slipped out without thought, and then my brain caught up. I was absolutely happy to help Luna out, and it wasn't as though we'd planned anything more than dinner. But I hadn't seen Anne and Sadie alone for a couple of weeks. "If Sadie is okay with it."

"She will be," Anne said.

As okay with it as Anne was. Because co-opting our girls' night out meant neither of them had to give up any more time with their men. I hated the bitter thought. "Cool. Let me know for sure, and I'll tell Violet."

"Are you okay? You sound... sad." Anne's tone shifted in an instant.

I smiled at my kitchen, to force the same feeling into my voice. "I'm great."

"You sure?"

"Positive."

"Okay. Call me if you need to talk, and we'll see you Saturday night."

My expression slipped the instant I disconnected. Anne was busy with work. Her shorter hours meant no weekend work, not that she had unlimited time.

Why was her time with me so much easier to surrender than her time with her guys?

Probably not a fair question—that wasn't why Anne made the request.

Was I sure?

I was practiced at bottling my hurt and redirecting it into work. I didn't quite have the same willpower when it came to other things, and the next morning, my order from my dairy distributor included a tub of cherry-chunk, brownie batter delight ice cream. Which I spent the next two nights making an unhealthy dent in, as a dinner replacement.

By Friday night, I'd eaten way more than I intended to, but that didn't stop me from serving up another big bowl. I put a banana in there—that made it healthy, right?

I was binge-watching Project Runway, waiting for the inevitable moment when the token Plus Size model would be eliminated, when an unknown number rang through on my cell phone.

Not unusual, since I used the phone for business. I summoned my inner customer service persona, and swiped to answer. "This is Jaelyn."

"Don't hang up, please."

All the ice cream in the world couldn't suffocate the hurt Owen's voice summoned. I was too frozen to speak or disconnect. If I said anything, I wouldn't be able to hide how I felt, and he wasn't worth the tirade that wanted to push past my lips.

"Lyn?"

"My friends call me Lyn, you don't." I kept my voice steel. "I'm not signing your contract."

"That's not why I'm calling. I want to apologize."

"There's nothing to apologize for. We all know what happened. I would have preferred to know up front I was part of the business transaction, so I'd know I was a whore." I winced at the emotion that leaked into my words.

"Technically we were the ones exchanging sex for what we wanted. But we weren't—"

My fury spiked. "Are you actually mansplaining *my own feelings* to me?"

"I'm sorry. That wasn't my intent." Owen sounded sincere. Then again, he had yet to sound otherwise. "And sex plus a business proposition wasn't either. I didn't go into that thinking *If we fuck, that'll make negotiations easier.*"

"Uh-huh."

"Neither did Kingston. He's a good guy."

Why hadn't I hung up yet? Because he didn't get to see how pissed off I was. "He is your business partner." Friend? Lover? I'd never actually clarified that, but it didn't matter. "It might not be a great relationship if you didn't think highly of him." I bit back my thoughts about Kingston trying too hard, in order to hide his insecurities. "Let me guess, he just has a hard time separating business and pleasure. Did you know who I was at the coffee shop?"

"No."

"Really." My tone was back to flat.

"I swear to you."

A clipped laugh slipped out. "Your word doesn't mean anything to me."

asking for it

"That's fair." Owen let out a long exhale. "Listen, forget the pitch. Come up to the reservoir with us this weekend."

Seriously? My disbelief and distrust couldn't crank any higher. "Why?"

"You'll like these people, not just as connections, but as people. And I had fun the other day, we'd like to spend time with you again."

Uh-huh. "What's your end game?" I didn't understand any of this, including why I hadn't hung up yet. Oh, right, because I wasn't letting him see that I cared.

"As in, what am I hoping to achieve?"

"Exactly that. Is this the next attempt to lull me into a false sense of security, and then dump another *you won't want to turn this down* pitch on me? Tug at my emotions to get me to play?" My experiences said that was the only reason for someone to keep trying this hard to win me over—they wanted something.

"Do I strike you as a *tug on emotions* kind of guy?" Owen asked flatly.

Mister Infuriating Logic? "No."

"My *end game* is spending more time with you. And as Kingston would say, enjoying the view. We'll pick you up at six Sunday morning."

"I haven't said yes, and I'm not up that early on a Sunday anyway."

"You are, because you bake everything fresh the same day."

Logical prick. I did still want to meet his friends. It may not do me any good, if this was some sort of cruel prank—my gut curdled at the idea mixed with memories. But if he was sincere, I may have a way to easily take care of this zoning thing, and if it was a joke, they'd never know they had any impact on me. I knew how to grin through the worst.

"Are you in?" Owen asked. "I should warn you, we're not giving up on your café, but I'll find a different way to convince you, and it won't involve tricks or sex or asking over and over again."

"I'm curious to see how what you think will work." And I was ready to turn him down, regardless.

"Me too. Sunday at six?"

He wasn't getting the best of me. Telling him *no* felt like the easy out. I was going to make them work for a result they weren't going to get. "I'll be ready."

Chapter Eight

Saturday night, Anne was already at the restaurant when I arrived five minutes early. So were Luna and Violet, but they stood several feet away from Anne.

I tugged them all together, and made introductions. I'd met Luna a few times, but she tended to be quiet unless she was talking about topics she was passionate about.

Sadie showed up just a few minutes later. "Oh, come on," she called lightly as she approached. "I was even on time. Do you know anyone else who's not early to everything?"

"Fashionably tardy is one of your charms," I teased.

Sadie stuck her tongue out at me and flipped me off. "Two minutes early is not late."

"Come on." Anne grabbed my arm. "I skipped lunch. I'm starved."

"How did you skip… Oh. Chase is out of town, isn't he?" I put the pieces together. She needed a Chase in her life to keep her fed, she was so skinny.

That was the last thing I needed in mine. A man who wanted me to eat more. Lunch with Owen and Kingston rushed back, rapidly followed by the memories of amazing sex, and asinine things said after.

Tomorrow was only to make connections.

We were shown to a table, and conversation was stuttered as we ordered drinks and food. I wasn't in the mood for Sadie and Anne to give me *looks* for getting a salad, so I indulged with quesadillas, and asked for a box, so I could put half of it aside immediately.

As our food arrived, things relaxed.

Anne and Luna slid into more technical conversation, filled with terms I only understood in the loosest sense. They were swapping programming stories and, from the laughs, jokes in a literal different language.

I'd never seen Luna this interactive. It made me smile that she and Anne were getting along so well.

"You obviously know your shit. What do you need me for?" Anne dipped a fry in enough ranch dressing to drown it, and popped the food in her mouth.

"I can't get anyone to talk to me. Like, interviewers and such." Luna pushed her food around her plate.

asking for it

She could be some serious competition for me when it came to picking-but-not-eating.

Anne tilted her head and studied Luna. "What's your specialty?"

"Network security." Luna's enthusiasm for high-level java jokes vanished beneath a soft voice.

Violet nudged her. "She's the best. Seriously. She did this thing with my VPN… Am I allowed to tell them about that?"

Luna nodded. "Only them."

"She did this thing where… hell, she basically rewrote it, and now I can watch K-Dramas as they air."

"You don't speak Korean." Not that I was aware of, anyway.

Violet grinned. "No, but I can infer a lot from what's happening on the screen."

"Jealous." Sadie's tone was playful. "You can hook me up, Luna? Pretty please with sugar on top?"

Pink dotted Luna's cheeks, but she smiled. "Sure."

"I can talk to our security guy, see if he has any referrals for you," Anne said.

Luna's eyes grew wide. "No. That's okay. Taurus is… I mean, really, it's fine. Don't worry about it."

I wasn't understanding this conversation for entirely different reasons than I didn't understand the programming one. Rinslet's head of network security was Zane. "What's Taurus?"

"Never mind." Luna ducked her head. What I thought was quiet before was practically shouting compared to her volume now. "I wasn't sure what I was hoping you could do for me, but don't worry about it."

I looked between Luna and Anne. "What did I miss?"

Anne paused, burger halfway to her mouth. "Zane was an old school hacker, and he went by Taurus."

"He's-the-best. Probably. Definitely." Luna's jumbled reply sounded defensive.

Pieces clicked in my head. How didn't I see it sooner? I loosely followed cybercrime, because I had to make sure my café was safe. A few years ago there was a huge FBI takedown that no one was talking about outside of those circles. A young woman who had supposedly written a piece of malware that brought an entire sector of the college system to its knees. "You were behind *Project Fail*."

"I wasn't *behind* it." And now it looked like Luna was trying to vanish inside herself. A move I was intimately familiar with. "I didn't mastermind it or anything. Someone paid me to do a job, it was a challenging one, and… I'd like to say I didn't know any better, but really my ego won out in the end, and

I convinced myself it would be okay, mostly because I wanted to prove to myself I could do it."

"Oh. Wow." Anne sounded awed. "That was you? You've got *mad* skills."

"I'm not doing that anymore, I swear," Luna said. "I've done good things since then, I promise. But now that past is linked to my name, and no one will talk to me."

"I'll ask around—without dropping names, and let you know what I find out, Luna," Anne said.

We drifted into silence as everyone ate, then Sadie turned to me. "Anne said you were all smiley the other day," she said.

Oh yeah, that. "Couple of cute guys at the bookstore were friendly and flirty. Nothing big, just the kind of attention that makes a woman smile." I stopped short of saying when, since I'd blown Anne and Sadie off to make that trip. I'd rather not get into details anyway, since thinking about the next day summoned a jumble of emotions that made my gut churn and my food suddenly unappetizing.

Sadie looked skeptical. *"Friendly and flirty?* Tell us more."

"There's nothing else to say, really. You don't want a play-by-play of them asking about my yaoi." My smile looked real, but I was being devoured from the inside-out.

Sadie's expression said *I really do*, but she nodded. "That's fair."

I might tell her and Anne later, but definitely not when anyone else could hear. It took me a long time to learn to open up to them, and even now there was a tiny nagging, every time I brought a problem to them, that said I was either being a bother, or was stupid if I couldn't figure out the solution on my own. Did I think the same of them? Of course not. My low self-esteem loved the boost of knowing I could help someone else.

"Ooh, speaking of"—Violet was suddenly excited—"what ended up happening with those two guys the other day? The ones who came into the shop. I'm surprised they haven't been back. Disappointed, really. They were *hot*." She made a sizzling sound.

"They were assholes." I needed to change the subject, but was drawing a blank. My brain had chosen to focus on the parts of that day that didn't bother me—the kisses, the touches, the fun…

Sadie leaned in. "There were guys? Since when does asshole matter if you're only looking?"

She was throwing my own logic at me, damn it. I had a counter, though. "They're the guys who keep trying to buy my shop."

asking for it

"And they had the nerve to approach you in person?" Anne's cheerful demeanor slipped. "You want I should hunt them down?"

It's okay. We talked. We fucked. They're still assholes, but I was an idiot, so it's not their fault. I wanted to spill, so badly, but not in front of Violet and Luna. They were sweet enough, but they weren't my inner circle. "No, but thank you. It's one of those too-weird-for-fiction stories. There was a disaster while they were there, they helped, and at the end of the night"—they showed their true colors—"they promised to back off on the *we want your business* thing." The lie tasted as bad as the memory.

"They've been calling you for more than a year," Sadie said. "Why would they back off now, all the sudden?"

They wouldn't. I shrugged, not having a better response.

The conversation shifted away from me, and kept going for a few hours. As the clock crept toward ten, my tomorrow-plans loomed like a big, daunting beacon in my thoughts. I hated to be the one to leave first, but I needed to at least try to get some sleep before tomorrow. I pushed back from the table. "I hate to do this, but I've got an early morning. Are you all okay if I cut out early?"

"We'll be fine," Sadie said.

"What she said." Violet nodded at her.

Everyone was friends with everyone. Awesome. I looked at Sadie and Anne. "I'll call you Monday."

As I headed to my car, I heard footsteps running to catch up with me. "Lyn." Anne grabbed my arm to stop me. "Early morning? What's up?"

"Nothing. I promise." *Everything.*

Anne tugged me away from the restaurant entrance, to sit on a bench around the side of the building. "Tell me," she said.

"I slept with them." The instant the confession slipped out, I braced myself for the judgment. Not because Anne ever had, but there was a first time for everything. "I mean, not slept, but there was sex, but first there was niceness, and they were so complimentary, and we were having fun, and then they ruined it. I'm such an idiot."

"You're not." Anne twisted her fingers with mine and squeezed gently.

I dragged in a deep breath. "I am. Because that's where I'm going in the morning."

"For more sex? I mean, if you're gagging them first… then they can't ruin it, right?"

A laugh slipped out without my permission. "They know the Millers. They're going to introduce me. I'm going so they don't know they pissed me off, and so I can make friends with people on the city council. Not for sex."

"I can still hurt them for you, if you want."

"I'm good, but thank you."

Anne squeezed again. "I don't want to see you hurt. Ever. Pretty sure you told me something similar not too long ago, and it works both ways. If you're okay with all of this, then that's fine. But you're not an idiot. Do you have this under control, or do you want me to yank you out of it?"

I appreciated having the options. "I've got it under control." And the more times I told myself that, the truer it would be.

Chapter Nine

Leaving the restaurant before everyone else didn't help me when I got home; I tossed and turned most of the night.

When my doorbell rang in the morning, I was on round five billion of *what the hell am I doing*? The question hadn't stopped me from stuffing a swimsuit, towel, and change of clothes—none of which I intended to need—into an oversized bag, along with a bottle of Sauvignon Blanc, to go with brunch, or just picnic-style drinking in general.

I answered the door to find Kingston kneeling on the front step, head bowed.

He didn't look up. "I'm so, so sorry. Please forgive?"

Was I more embarrassed for him or me? I was at least a little curious if he could see up my denim skirt. "Please get up."

"I'd make a joke about being up just because you're here, but no erection humor until you forgive me." He stood, putting him a few inches above eye level instead of tantalizingly below.

asking for it

"Where's your other half?" I wasn't getting dragged into fun with him. No witty banter. No teasing.

Kingston patted his legs and chest, his back and front, and his left and right shoulder. "All of me is here."

"I meant Owen."

"Ah. He's in the car. Said watching me humiliate myself in front of you once fills out his lifetime quota."

I wasn't going to forgive him just because he was goofy and cute. "Anyone can grovel."

"But how many people do so willingly?"

I pursed my lips and stared at him.

"I'm sorry about the other day. Sincerely and honestly." His serious tone replaced the playfulness, and he held my gaze. "It may surprise you to hear this, but I don't always read a room right, and sometimes my jokes fall flat."

"If that's your idea of a joke… Has it ever in your life been appropriate to fuck someone and then tease them about it being for business?"

He shrugged, and pulled off *sheepish* with flair. "It's never come up before. You're unique in a lot of ways. Forgive me."

"Are you going to give up on trying to make the deal?"

"No."

The honesty was refreshing. I didn't like his answer, but I wouldn't have believed him if he said anything else.

"And fair warning in that same vein," Kingston said. "I'm hoping if you spend time with us, you'll see what a good idea this partnership is."

"What you're proposing isn't a partnership." It was pretending to let me stay on in a management position until they didn't like my feedback. I would only have the power they assigned me, that they could take away just as easily.

"Semantics. But I swear to you, cross my heart, hope to die, stick a needle in my eye swear to you, sex is not part of that equation. Anything physical is its own separate thing."

He wasn't talking past tense. But he was still being honest.

"In that case, I should be up front and say the only reason I'm going with you today is because"—someone's fucking with my zoning… I wasn't going to tell him that, in case he decided to use it as leverage—"you're right that it's good to make connections."

Kingston offered his arm. "That's fair. Shall we?"

My body wanted that contact again. That heat I felt every time he touched me. My heart and mind knew better. I Ignored his arm and fell into step beside him as we walked to the SUV waiting at the curb.

Owen smiled as we drew closer, and offered a cheerful "Morning," when we were within earshot.

"Morning." I tried to keep my tone and expression cool, but my smile was as genuine as it was hesitant.

Kingston held open the front passenger door for me.

"I'm fine in the back," I said.

"Take the seat." Kingston gestured. "He and I see each other all the time. If you're up here, it'll be harder for you to pretend you're not part of the conversation."

Called out on an intention I hadn't vocalized to myself. "Fine. Thank you."

We settled into our seats and hit the road. This early on a Sunday, there was no traffic, and we were on the freeway heading east in less than ten minutes.

"Are the two of you from Las Vegas originally?" I asked. It was where they opened their first store, and I'd rather lead the conversation toward them then let it drift back to me. If I gave them the right opening, they had the kind of egos that would let them talk for hours about themselves.

"No," Owen said.

I waited for more. So much for my brilliant plan and observations. It was early, though. I'd come up with something else to draw them out.

Kingston leaned forward, resting one arm on the center console between Owen and me. "Vegas was a twenty-first birthday present from my mother." Some of his cheer had vanished. This wasn't the business-voice I heard on the phone, but it wasn't his standard lightheartedness either. Odd way to sound when talking about family.

My parents were amazingly supportive, but I understood not everyone's were. I heard the same tone from Anne when she delved into her past.

"Fortunately"—Kingston's cheer was back, like flipping a switch—"I got to take my best buddy, and we tore up the town." He slapped Owen lightly on the arm.

"Ah. A fun-filled weekend of strippers, free booze, and high roller suites?" I kept my tone playful.

Owen laughed. It was a throaty joy that danced over me with temptation. It didn't matter that I barely knew him, I suspected that kind of amusement wasn't typical for him.

Which was fortunate, given how much I liked it.

"*Birthday Trip* is a code word for business trip, in this case. I was supposed to…"

asking for it

When Kingston didn't finish the thought, I glanced at him to see if I'd missed something. He'd leaned back in his seat, and was sitting with his face just out of my view.

"… find some direction," he finally said.

What made him hesitate? Did I want to know *that* much about them?

"We stumbled on a little gaming café," Owen said. "Most incredible thing we'd ever seen."

Kingston resumed his leaned forward position. "That's where we went instead of all that stuff you said. We spent days on end in that place."

I liked the visual, Kingston in a faded concert T-shirt, Owen in a button-down with the sleeves rolled up, both of them hunched over computers in someone else's shop, kicking ass in something multi-player.

"What's with the smile?" Own asked.

Was I? "You're not my typical customers." Why didn't I just tell them the truth? *I'm fantasizing about the two of you having fun, and it's both completely non-sexual and makes you even more desirable.* That was why.

"I think you'd be surprised. But this was also ten years ago." Owen was sliding into the more casual tone I'd heard from him when we were baking together.

They were either supremely confident in their plan to win me over, or capable of letting down their walls a lot more easily than I did. What would it be like, to be so comfortable with existing? I shook the deep thought aside. "I know how the story goes from here—you spend time in the shop, you think *this is wicked awesome*, and set up your own place to drive the guy out of business."

"Ouch. And no." The look Owen gave me was withering.

"He was already going out of business, which we found out after chatting him up," Kingston said.

A process I was becoming familiar with. The two of them were practiced at the *chatting someone up* experience. "About twenty minutes, then?" Please let this joke land better than my previous comment.

Kingston grinned. "Young and not nearly so experienced, remember? More like an hour."

I laughed.

"The shop owner mentioned things were failing." Owen picked up the story. "I was straight out of cooking school, and every one of my business ideas centered on baking, so I tossed out some ideas about fresh baked sweets."

"He liked what we had to say, but wanted to move onto other things." The way Kingston dove in, it felt like they'd rehearsed this story. They probably had, but the two of them still had a dynamic that was nice to watch. "He's an old school, hard core gamer who didn't like the direction of the industry, or that his shop couldn't make it as-is."

"So he sold it to us." Owen glanced at Kingston in the rearview mirror.

What was that look? Questioning? About what?

Kingston shrugged. "Everyone already knows, she might as well too." He focused on me. "I did it to piss off my mother. She'd told me to make something of my life, and I intended to prove I could do that through gaming. Not as direct a route as some people take, but I'm happy with the outcome."

"And the rest is history and listed for the world to read on our website." Owen wrapped the entire tale up with a nice neat bow.

A story like theirs didn't end so abruptly, though. I could ask for more info—it was tempting— but I didn't want to delve into the innermost details of their private lives. I wasn't here to get to know them on a friendship level, just to learn enough to protect myself and my own shop.

"So are the two of you…" What was I doing? This was the exact opposite of not delving into their private lives.

Owen glanced at me. "Are we…?"

It wasn't that I had a problem asking *are you a couple*? They'd played tonsil tag in front of me, so it was a reasonable assumption. "I'm wondering if your partnership goes beyond business. Beyond friendship.”

Silence.

I glanced between them. “Is this another of those *secrets* like how long you’ll be in town?”

“No. Rather, it’s not something we talk about a lot, but it’s not a secret,” Kingston said. “It’s just not as cut and dried as a label.”

“Also, I don’t want you to take it wrong when I say the kiss the other day was as much for your benefit as ours,” Owen added.

Curious. “Now you have to explain.”

Kingston drummed his fingers on the center console.

“You said you had a friend, the one who got you the X poster, and the two of you make better friends than lovers.” Owen seemed to be measuring his words. “It’s kind of like that.”

Kingston silently flattened his palm on the leather. “*Kind of.* I dated this woman, years ago, who thought it would be hot to see two guys together. That was the first time we…”

“Shared.” Owen picked up the thread without pause. “There was kissing, more, between Kingston and me. It was good.”

“Good isn’t exactly a screaming endorsement. And doesn’t quite line up with that kiss I saw.” It had been incredible for me, and I’d only watched.

asking for it

"He's understating things," Kingston said. "Tell me you're surprised. She and I didn't last long—she was jealous of my relationship with Owen—"

"Seriously?" I shouldn't be any more surprised about that than Owen being minimalist in his description. But it had been her idea.

Kingston playfully tapped Owen on the arm. "I was glad it showed early. My friendship with Owen is one of those things I'm not sacrificing. We've got an occasional with-benefits thing going on. We lean into the passion when it feels right for the situation."

"You were reading yaoi, you're an X fan, the kiss added to the moment." Owen made it sound like a reasonable step in a business plan, rather than an intense, shared moment.

Right. "But it was totally spontaneous." I kept my sarcasm light.

"We didn't discuss it first, if that's what you're implying." Kingston almost sounded wounded. He didn't have the right.

But I liked the idea that they were in-tune enough with each other that a kiss could be spontaneous, and my imagination was running rampant with fantasies of them together. Especially given how easily they talked about being friends-with-sometimes-benefits.

"You're not jealous, are you?" The faintest hint of concern ran through Kingston's voice.

I'd wonder if I'd imagined it, but his tone wasn't hard to read.

"We're not dating." I had to remind myself as much as him. "But no." Kind of turned on. Okay, a lot turned on. Letting that truth slip out was a gaping chasm of a line that I wasn't crossing with them.

Chapter Ten

The cabin was rustically beautiful, as I expected from a group of twenty to thirty something trust fundies. In the middle of a forest clearing, set back far enough from the lake to be private, but close enough to have its own dock, and make swimming and boating convenient.

The interior defied the log-cabin look, with tile floors, stainless appliances, and high-end electronics. I wasn't judging—it looked comfortable, and it was hard to complain about that.

Kingston and Owen introduced me to the six other people there. Half had just come back from an unsuccessful morning of fishing, and the other three were arguing over how many ingredients could change in a drink and still have it be a mimosa.

The morning passed in a blur of fruit plates and idle chatter. The more time that ticked away, the further I drifted toward the living room walls.

I should mingle. This wasn't a large group, and I *was* here to make connections. The way everyone had split off into packs of two or three made it difficult to know where to gravitate, so the edge of the room got my company.

"Mind if I share your wall?" Owen startled me when he brushed my shoulder and leaned back next to me. He handed me a cold bottle of water. "I'm sorry for assaulting you with so many names at once. It's a lot to keep track of."

I took a long swallow of water. The icy cold froze my uncertainty. I looked up to find Owen watching me. I turned away before eye contact could become more. "It's fine. I'm good with names."

"I should have guessed that. Let's see… you give each one of them a nickname, and associate their real names with whomever you've decided they are?"

I didn't like being pegged so easily, even if it was exactly what I was doing with everyone else in the room. "Maybe."

"Care to share?"

"No."

"Why not?" Kingston seemed to appear from nowhere, and planted himself between us and the rest of the room.

"People never appreciate the instant judgment, even when there's truth to it," Owen said. "So many want to categorize everything around them with neat little labels, but apply one of those labels to them…"

asking for it

It was both terrifying and enticing that he understood where I was coming from. "What he said. And if I picked the wrong trait to focus on with your friends, I'll find myself walking home."

"Never." Kingston didn't look fazed. So, status quo. "But people, am I right?" He rolled his eyes, but never stopped smiling.

I gave an exaggerated sigh. "It's true. Life would be so much easier if it came with anime narration that explained every single intent and power—"

"In excruciating detail?" Owen pushed away from the wall to look at me. "You want a diatribe about everything except the one thing that matters?"

"Which is?" I had to know.

"*I like you, let's fuck,*" Owen said. "When was the last time you heard anyone say that in an anime who wasn't cast as the overbearing love interest?"

"I've all but said that, what does that make me?" Kingston asked.

Far more appealing than he should be. "The enemy," I teased. "I take back what I said. Endless grandstanding and super villain monologuing suck."

Kingston rested a finger under my chin and raised my gaze to his. "You don't get out of it that easily. I like you. Let's fuck."

Heat flooded me, and I broke the connection. It severed the spark flowing between us, and I instantly wanted that feeling back. "You like my café. We're not going to screw. And you're definitely not what snap judgment says you are. Neither of you."

"Is that good or bad?" Kingston asked.

I didn't know yet. "It's certainly interesting."

"I'll take interesting. Life can always use another surprise." Condensation had formed on Owen's bottle, and when he tiled his head back to drink, several drops ran down his chin, over his throat, and dampened his shirt enough to tease.

Kingston dragged his thumb over Owen's chin, wiping away some of the water.

Thirsty took on a literal form as I suppressed the desire to lean in draw my tongue along a similar path. I had male friends who were close to the point of playful flirting, and I'd never seen them do anything that intimate. "Not all surprises are good." I pressed my own water bottle to my cheek. Dribbles hit my chest, and both their gazes followed. I wanted to turn in on myself and hide, but I pretended not to notice.

"Agree to disagree." Owen looked me in the eye again. "Even the bad kind of unexpected leads to change and growth."

I couldn't argue that, but it didn't make me like the idea of bad surprises any more than I had thirty seconds ago. "Change can be scarring." Sometimes those scars were invisible. I certainly went out of my way to hide mine.

"Come join us." Peter interrupted, saving me from my thoughts, and pulled us into their group of two. "We want your opinion on this start-up coming out of Phoenix. The newest *we'll beat Facebook* site."

They didn't want my opinion, or Kingston's it seemed. They were mostly interested in what Owen had to say. I wasn't surprised they ignored me, but how surprised would they be to know Kingston had more to offer than he let on.

We moved between groups for several hours. Lunch was an informal buffet of more fresh fruit. I was grateful for that on a lot of levels. And by that afternoon, I found myself in a lawn chair, in a small clearing a bit back from the lake. The trees blocked the sun, and the cool breeze was enough to tease the heat from my skin.

Owen and Kingston were with me. They hadn't left my side much, which was odd since we were here to see their friends, but I was grateful at not being left to fend for myself. What was I thinking? I wasn't the kind of person who mingled and made connections.

We had company, though, and it was exactly who I needed it to be. Ravyn had been my favorite person to talk to so far, aside from my not-dates, and her brother Ramsey was on the city council.

"What do you do, Lyn?" Ravyn asked.

Enjoying her company didn't mean I'd completely shed my discomfort in this group. I didn't want them to see they intimidated me at all. "I'm an entrepreneur."

"She owns *Loading Java*," Ramsey said.

Ravyn gave him a curious look. "How do you know that?"

"I saw the zoning order come across my desk."

He was definitely the guy for me to meet. This day wasn't a mistake after all.

I glanced at Owen and Kingston, both looking relaxed, gorgeous, and frequently focused on me. I had a hard time thinking it was a mistake anyway, no matter how much I shouldn't be fantasizing about them. It wasn't like I was planning a future with them, though. I simply liked the memories of all the different things they did with their fingers… tongues… other extremities.

"I've always wanted to drop in there, and I'm not sure why I haven't. Why a gaming café?" Ravyn set her beer on the ground, and scooted forward on her chair. The way she leaned in, elbows on her knees, pressed her breasts together. Stunning view. I wasn't sure if I wanted to stare, or wallow in envy.

The fact that no one else gave her a second glance was odd, but not bad for my self-esteem.

"For the prestige and fame." I tossed out the joke lightly. *Please don't let it fall flat.*

asking for it

Kingston snickered.

Ravyn and Ramsey smiled.

"You may be in the wrong business," Ravyn said. "Only reason I know these assholes is they're friends with Ramsey."

"They're not big L.A. Players?" I feigned shock. "They told me they were invited to *every* party in Hollywood." Except I hadn't had a clue what they looked like until they walked into my shop.

The teasing earned me more chuckles. I liked having a similar sense of humor to these people.

"Property values in L.A. are outrageous. We're not going near that place." Leave it to Owen to pick the reasonable retort.

Another thing that made him sexy.

And I could stop drooling over them any time now, please. "I love gaming, anime and baking… and I found a way to do all three." My story sounded a lot like Kingston and Owen's. Instinct braced me for a jab or two about *of course you love baking, it shows.*

"I need to stop by at some point," Ramsey said. "What's your specialty? Like, if I have to order just one thing off the menu, what do I get?"

"It's all good." My inner fat-girl was still on alert for the jokes. *Of course you like it all.*

Ravyn slapped him on the leg. "She's not going to sell if she thinks it sucks, dummy."

Ramsey shrugged. "Of course not, but she's got a favorite. Don't you?" He looked at me.

"The chocolate croissant. Messy, but worth it." And the creation I was proudest of. The recipe took a lot of trial and error.

"Messy as in, chocolate everywhere? All over your fingers…?" Kingston wiggled his eyebrows.

I fixed him with a warning glare, and braced myself for a surge of bad feelings associated with sucking chocolate off fingers. But everything that led up to his damning question at the end of that night was still a pleasant memory. "All over."

Ravyn cleared her throat. "I was thinking it was too cold to go in the water, but someone needs to cool off."

"You can't take the heat of this package." Kingston gestured at himself.

I was certainly struggling with it.

Ravyn rolled her eyes, stood, and offered me a hand. "Do you want to walk away from this testosterone fest, or stay and be worshiped?"

"They're not—" Not me. I was never the center of that kind of attention.

Ravyn pursed her lips. "They are."

"I could use a drink." I stood as well.

Ravyn gestured toward the cabin, and we headed into the kitchen. She grabbed two lemonades from the fridge and handed me one.

"How well do you know them? Owen and Kingston?" I tried to sound casual. I sipped my drink to hide any fidgeting.

"They've been friends with Ramsey for years. I see them every few months."

I both did and didn't want to ask my next question. It would be obvious why I wondered, but since Ravyn already made the comment about worshiping, it wasn't as though she'd missed the attraction. "Do you know…" How should I phrase this? "Do they ever mix business with pleasure?"

"No." There was no hesitation in her response. "I mean, I guess it's possible, since I don't know how they spend their downtime, but I can't imagine Owen *ever* crossing that line. He doesn't even like to call in favors."

"They never do." Ramsey's reply came from the kitchen doorway. "I'd bet a hedge fund on that. Kingston blurs a few lines, but—if you don't already know this, you haven't spent enough time with them—their business is their world. They'd never jeopardize it."

I understood the sentiment, but was I doing exactly that to myself, by being here?

Chapter Eleven

By the end of the night, as we were saying our *goodbyes*, I'd decided to forgive Kingston for joking that sex meant I'd sell my business to them. It was a lot less stressful to go back to enjoying the scenery and the conversation, at least for the next hour or so drive down the canyon.

After that, it wouldn't matter. Our time together would be done.

When we reached the SUV, Kingston playfully tugged my arm toward the back seats. "Let Owen chauffeur."

"That seems a little odd." Didn't it?

Owen shrugged. "No odder than the two of us in the front seat and Kingston alone in back. Keep each other company."

As we headed toward main roads, an unexpected sadness surged through me, clenching around my heart.

"Why the frown?" Kingston tugged a thumb over my bottom lip.

asking for it

The intimate touch caught me off-guard, but soothed me. Did I dare say out loud what I was thinking? It would be rude to hide it. "I'm not ready for the day to end."

Insecurities twinged inside. Was it stupid to admit that?

The corner of Kingston's mouth tugged up. "It's not over yet. Don't waste the drive pouting."

"What would you suggest instead?" I asked.

He trailed his fingers up the inside of my thigh, and fissures of need sparked under my skin. "You look gorgeous in this skirt." He wasn't answering my question, but I could be patient. "I swear I had a *Basic Instinct* moment every time you crossed or uncrossed your legs today."

"Except, I'm not a killer." I knew where the compliment was going, but it was tinged. "Or… whatever. I've never actually seen the movie."

"The important thing is, you're *way* more attractive than Sharon Stone." Kingston's fingers crept higher, nudging my legs apart.

I shook my head. "I'm not."

"Disagree." Kingston moved his hand further up the inside of my thighs, and my skirt crept higher.

That same nervous *we're in public* fear was back. But it was dark, the windows were tinted, and there was no one else on the road.

Kingston brushed a light touch over my panties, and I gasped.

"Is that a *keep going?*" He asked.

Was it? Just a few days ago I was furious with him. With both of them. Was I willing to dive into a physical situation again? Kingston told me up front, his goal was to prove they were likeable business partners.

Did that include the sex?

"Lyn?" Concern crept into Kingston's voice.

I was spread-legged, skirt bunched around my hips, while one man drove and another teased me. "I don't want this to end like the other night." I kept my voice firm, trying to make the words sound like a command more than a terrified confession.

"I don't either." Kingston eased his hand back, resting it on my knee instead. "This isn't… It's sex. Not business."

That simplified things. Didn't it? I glanced up at Owen. "Are just going to drive and pretend there's nothing going on back here?" I tried to keep my tone light.

"I'm not pretending anything." He briefly met my gaze in the rear-view mirror. "I'm listening to and enjoying every second of it."

Being watched wasn't my thing. Not even by whomever I was with at the time. So why did the fact that Owen was the watcher—listener—raise goosebumps everywhere?

"How many times have you done this?" I asked. The situation was too well orchestrated.

Kingston squeezed my knee. "This specifically? You'd be my first. You get to pop my fooling-around-in-the-back-seat-while-my-best-friend-drives cherry."

I did want it. *Him.* Twice with the same fling broke a rule I'd rarely had to consider, but it wasn't as though we'd make a habit of this. I could think of the drive home as a chance to rewrite the ending of our last hook-up.

After tonight, I wouldn't put myself in a social situation with them again. Easy to do given they didn't live here.

I summoned the boldness that acted as my shield when I went to bars, covered Kingston's hand, and slid it up my leg again. "Yes. Keep going."

"Face me." He lightly slapped the inside of my thigh.

The teasing sting made me sigh. I shifted in the seat, one knee bent between us and the other foot on the floor.

Kingston leaned in and kissed me so lightly, I felt his breath on my skin as much as his touch. "Nope, not enough," he growled.

He pressed his weight into me when he slanted his mouth over mine. I half-reclined against the door and my body molded to his. He deepened the kiss, drawing it out until I felt the tingles all the way to my toes.

Kingston trailed his fingers down my chest, and followed the same path with his mouth, passing my skirt, and skipping the pulse of need between my legs, to tease along the inside of my thighs instead.

I writhed under the playfully light touch, shifting my hips to bring me closer to his mouth.

He chuckled against my skin, and pressed a palm into my stomach to keep me from moving.

It was the most delicious torture.

Kingston finally moved back up, to scrape his teeth over the crotch of my panties.

I whimpered.

He hooked his fingers in the elastic, and dragged the lingerie down my legs. When he dragged his tongue up my slit, I gasped and my hips bucked, needing more.

He devoured me with a hunger that made my pulse scream. Licking along my slick skin, diving his tongue inside me to taste my inner walls. Groaning as loudly as I was. He moved his fingers to my clit.

My entire body jerked in response.

The longer he stayed between my legs, the more the outside world fell away. My breath came in pants, and I gripped his short hair, needing something to hold onto and not wanting him to stop.

I came hard. My hips bucked, and my entire body tensed for a moment, before I slumped back with a happy sigh.

Kingston climbed back up my body, and dropped his mouth on mine again, kissing me hard, sharing my taste with me.

I wasn't ready for this to end. I reached below his waist to trace the hard bulge in his jeans. His muffled moan against my mouth was electricity sliding over me. Still teasing his erection, I pressed my body into his, to push us both upright, until he was sitting and I knelt next to him.

The more intently I stroked through denim, the louder he groaned. I liked that sound. The hum against my lips.

I liked orgasms as much as the next person, but I enjoyed giving as much as receiving. There was a unique rush in seeing another person get off, especially when I was helping or even better, responsible.

I dragged down Kingston's zipper and freed him. His skin was hot against my palm as I stroked. When I lowered my head and flicked my tongue over the head of his cock, he sucked in a sharp breath through his teeth.

Incredible sound, and delicious motivation to take more than a taste. I took him into my mouth, sucking, licking, and pumping. Each jerk of his body and growl of pleasure was an invisible touch, dancing through over me.

He reached under my chest, between my legs, staying away from my still-tender clit, and sliding along my slick skin.

Desire, the volume of his moans, and the ambient need drove my pace. I lost myself in sounds and sensations as he thrust against the back of my throat. I whimpered when he slipped two fingers inside me.

The angle and sensation weren't right to make me come, but I liked the feeling of penetration. That combined with the jerk of his hips spurred me on.

"Lyn." Kingston's voice was gravel. "Gorgeous. I'm too close." He tried to nudge me back.

I was wrapped in the moment and didn't want to stop.

He slid his fingers higher, to my clit, and a shudder of *too much* mingled with *don't stop* and stalled my brain.

Another orgasm rushed over me, flashing a rainbow of stars behind my eyelids. I gasped in the pleasure, until my body jerked away from his touch.

asking for it

Kingston's chuckle was self-satisfied as his hand fell away.

I was lost in the haze of climax, and not done with him yet. I resumed stroking and licking. Bobbing my head. I wanted to taste him. Hear that enticing sound he made when he came.

And it was loud. His grunts increasing in volume as he thrust against my face.

I didn't pull away as he finished. When he finally slowed to a stop, I licked him clean.

I knelt upright.

Kingston captured the back of my neck and crushed his mouth to mine. There was no tender sweetness here. He consumed me, diving into the kiss like he was as desperate to be close as I was. This kind of intensity and need could burn me alive, and I'd love every minute of it.

When we finally broke apart, I was breathless. Flushed. Just plain happy.

"That was possibly the single hottest thing I've ever heard." Owen's comment startled me.

Kingston kissed my forehead and squeezed my hand. "I have a singularly hot partner," he said.

I'd almost forgotten Owen was here. That we were driving down the freeway at seventy miles an hour. That anything else existed. I wanted to be embarrassed, but a new layer of pleased wove with everything else, that Owen had been listening.

After we straightened our clothing enough to sit, I leaned into Kingston for the rest of the ride home, ignoring the whisper in the back of my mind insisting I was going to miss this. It was a fling like any other, and this was my chance to burn the good into my mind, and let it keep me warm until the next hookup.

When we turned onto my street, I forced all the emotion from my veins.

Owen opened the rear SUV door, and offered his hand. I accepted, but Kingston wrapped an arm around my waist before I could leave, and pulled me into his chest.

Owen grabbed Kingston's wrist, stepped close enough I felt his heat, and pressed Kingston's hand to the front of his jeans, to cup a bulge that was visible even in the dim lighting.

Hot.

"This is what the two of you do to me." Owen's even tone was a new caress that made my mind whimper and beg, and he hadn't touched me.

This was *friends with occasional benefits?* Because there was no way it was purely for my enjoyment.

"What are you going to do about it?" Kingston's retort was borderline bratty challenge.

Owen raised an eyebrow, and focused on me. "If I didn't have an early flight, I'd fuck this stunning woman and make you watch."

Yes, please. Though, *early flight* sounded like an excuse. I wouldn't be hurt. The three of us were screwing. The two of us? Owen had been there, watching, and for all I knew, that was how he sated an attraction to Kingston that neither of them wanted to label. But the fact that I didn't know proved what we all had was nothing more than sex. "So that's my answer?" I kept my tone light. "You're leaving tomorrow?"

"*He* has an early flight. You're not getting rid of me that easily." Kingston's breath was hot on the back of my neck.

Owen dropped Kingston's hand to squeeze my fingers. "Technically, neither of us is leaving for good. We want a shop here because we're moving here. I'm making a few stops at our other locations around the country, then I'll be back. You're not getting rid of us so easily."

But they weren't a couple, moving across the country together.

You don't have a shop here. If I brought that up, we'd be talking business as it related to us. I didn't want to spoil a second night in a row that way.

My brain was already racing ahead, though. Never seeing them again felt bad. Having to avoid them in the same city could be worse.

Because I was a novelty and a fetish. I was screwing out of my league, and I couldn't pretend otherwise much longer. Meeting their friends today reinforced that point too distinctly.

Worse though, I was starting to like Owen and Kingston. That was stupid and terrifying. "I won't keep you. I have an early day anyway." It was tricky to extract myself from their embrace with any manner of grace, but I managed to get my feet planted on the pavement, and put distance between me and them.

Kingston hopped from the back seat and reached for me.

I stepped away from him. "I had a lot of fun today. Thank you."

"Us too." His smile didn't reach his eyes.

That wasn't hurt. There was no way it could be.

They'd leave and go enjoy their lives, pretending whatever they wanted about their relationship with each other, and I hoped the next woman enjoyed it as much as I had.

Chapter Twelve

Raindrops slamming against my window woke me about two minutes before my alarm went off. It was gorgeously gray outside. I love the rain, but thank goodness it held off until this morning.

Yesterday lingered in my head as I got ready for the morning. As much as I wanted to file things in a *Pleasant Memories* folder, and move on, I couldn't get the highlights out of my head.

I grabbed a sweatshirt that hung low enough to cover my ass, so I could wear leggings. It didn't matter that it was one of the hottest months of the year—rain meant cool weather, which meant I could be comfortable and hide inside my clothes at the same time.

As I did the morning's baking, my mind was free to drift to Kingston and Owen. Every time I yanked my thoughts away from them, and tried to ponder anything else, even repeating my favorite recipes, the men meandered their way into my head.

I needed to occupy my mind more intently. I was doing a podcast today with *Roxie's Face For*

Radio. That would distract me from missing men I barely knew.

If the situation were different, if Owen and Kingston weren't trying to push me out of this place, I'd go out with them again, if they asked.

Not that they would. Which was good, because I wasn't a long term girl. Not for guys like them. Once they settled down, they'd end up with trophy wives, probably occasionally help each other jerk off in the hot tub, and attend parties like the one this weekend, but stuffier.

Did I really think that little of them, that they'd live their lives for money and public image?

I had to. Believing anything else was dangerous

I wrapped up my morning baking, chatted with Violet for a bit, and headed out to Roxie's.

I'd been on her show a few times since Sadie introduced us; it was always a lot of fun, was great promo for Loading Java, and didn't require me to be on camera. Roxie's staff animated every episode.

The recording was fun, but when it was over my thoughts were free to drift back to Owen and Kingston.

That needed to stop.

Pouring myself into work for the rest of the day helped, and by the time I climbed into bed, I was exhausted enough I slept hard.

asking for it

Tuesday morning the guys were still vivid in my thoughts. Seriously, what was up with my brain? I didn't linger on one-night stands.

Throughout the day, every time I talked to someone, performed a basic task, glazed Danishes, my brain would wonder what kind of commentary one of them would have. Kingston with a joke. Owen with a reasonable observation.

Who did that? Got hot and bothered over a guy who couldn't take life seriously and one who saw the world through a completely structured lens? Logic wasn't sexy.

Yes it is.

Sigh.

Wednesday was more of the same, but Roxie's podcast with me aired that morning, so having it playing in the café gave me a new point of focus.

Distraction didn't last long, though. If anything, my missing-the-guys feeling was getting more intense, rather than fading.

This was why I should never see a fling more than once. Give me a little attention, and I lapped it up and whined for more like a lovesick puppy.

The rain was back that night, and the white noise of falling water helped soothe my fractured thoughts. I wanted extra comfort this evening, so I pulled on my ultimate wrap-me-up-in-a-hug outfit. It was a kitten onesie Sadie gave me for my birthday.

She made it herself, which meant it fit perfectly, and was super soft and comfortable.

My phone rang and I glanced at it. Only friends got to talk to me this late.

Owen's name flashed on the screen.

I swore my heart started panting.

Send him to voicemail—that was the only answer.

I grabbed the phone and hit *Answer*. "This is Lyn."

"Can I call you Lyn? Are we friends now?" His voice was huskier than normal, like he was tired. Which must be why he was more playful than I was used to.

I let out an exaggerated sigh. "I guess I'll allow it tonight." It was easy to keep the teasing in my voice—I was so much happier to hear from him than I should be. I almost didn't care if he was calling to make a buy pitch.

Almost.

"In that case, Lyn, I called to tell you I caught the show today, with Roxie. You sounded fantastic."

My heart lapped up the simple praise, and my mind had lost any ground in the *stay removed* argument. It was going to make one final push anyway. "Did you tune in to make sure I *represented your future brand appropriately?*"

"Is that what you want me to say?"

asking for it

"Do I strike you as a *tell me what I want to hear* kind of person?" I playfully turned a version of his question from the other day back on him.

He chuckled. "Not even close. I turned it on to hear you—hand to God. If Kingston had told me you had such a sexy voice, even without the visuals..."

"You're one to talk." I didn't mean to let that slip, but this was too easy. "Pun not intended? Was that a pun?"

"If you stretch your imagination a little... Or a lot."

"I've got a pretty vivid imagination." Right now, for instance, it was whispering completely inappropriate things in my ear, in Owen's voice, while it pictured his fingers trailing over my body.

"I usually don't, but... Anyway, you sounded good."

What had he been going to say? "You can't leave it at that. But what?" I asked.

"It's not business related."

"That's not dispelling my curiosity."

"You were warned." The way he said *warned* added a new layer to the fantasy, that somehow led to my ass being slapped. "But my imagination runs rampant when I'm talking to you."

Me too. Great, my brain had sided with my body and heart now. "I was warned." This was when I should call it a night. Thank him for tuning into

Roxie, and hang up. I lay back in bed, phone to my ear. "How's... Where are you today?"

"Chicago. It's windy. You also don't strike me as a *let's discuss the weather* kind of person."

Only if I had to, and it was one of the last things I wanted to be doing with Owen. "Make a lot of assumptions about the kind of person I am?"

"No more than you make about me."

Touché. "What else have you assumed?"

"I assume you're in bed, wearing something that makes you look delectable— *Fuck,* I wasn't going to say that."

Heat flooded me. Flirt or shut him down? "No take backs." Like I was going to give myself any choice. "And you're right. My pussy is on display for anyone to see who walks in the room."

Nothing.

Did I just screw up big time?

"Show me." Owen's tone left no room for argument.

Which made me specifically want to argue, even just teasingly. "I don't send pictures of myself to *anyone*. But maybe, if you asked really nicely, I'd consider a neck-down shot?"

"I'd rather see your face."

"That doesn't sound like begging."

"Please." He even made a request sound like an order.

asking for it

I grinned in my empty room, at the smooth retort. "Those are my rules." If I dragged this out too long, the punchline wouldn't be funny. It might not be anyway, but I was willing to take the chance. "I guess I can make an exception for you, because you sound sexy when you're tired." I was getting bold. I tugged up the hood of my onesie and snapped a picture from the chest up. "Sent."

More silence greeted me. Then Owen chuckled. It was the kind of laugh that flowed over me like skilled fingers, raising goosebumps everywhere. "Absolutely stunning," he said. "Most gorgeous pussy I've ever seen."

"Right?" My smile grew.

"You're lucky I don't have a furry fetish, or I'd be jerking off right now."

My breath caught. Yeah, I'd opened the door with a pussy joke, but… "You mean that wasn't the plan?"

"The plan was to call and tell you I caught you on the show, make small talk, and then wish you a good rest of your evening."

"Except you're not a small talk person either."

"I'm really not."

One of the things that made him attractive beyond the *wow he's hot* level.

"I genuinely want to know how Chicago is," I said. "Do you have any free time when you make these trips? What will you do while you're there? Any places I have to see?"

"You're good at that."

At asking questions? Here was another one. "Good at what?"

"Not talking about yourself."

I hadn't intentionally steered the conversation away from me. Not this time. "I wasn't—"

"My point exactly." Owen sounded playful. "Have you ever been here?"

"No." I could stop there, but it wouldn't hurt me to offer a little more personal information. "Vacation when I was little was camping in Jackson Hole. I always said I'd travel when I got older, but first there was no money, and now there's work."

"You take vacations, though."

"Work, and still no money. And no, time off isn't really a thing I do." Had I just walked into a trap? Thanks, brain, for picking now to ignore the flirty fun. "Is this where you tell me if I sold to you, I'd have both time and money?"

"This is where I describe the scene from my hotel window, since you can't be here."

"I'd love that."

There was a pause with shuffling and what sounded like a sliding window or door in the background. "I've got a view of the river," Owen said. "The skyline here isn't like in Salt Lake, here you can see forever on a clear day. But from my room, it's more like a corridor lined with buildings and bright lights, cut out of black velvet, with a plush carpet of water running down the center."

The verbal tour would be fantastic on its own, but in Owen's voice it was almost foreplay. "You make it sound amazing."

"It is through the right lens. Add it to your bucket list."

"Is that an order?"

"You don't strike me as a *take orders* kind of woman."

I wasn't. "For the right person…"

"The right person wouldn't demand it of you." He was so reasonable.

I could talk to him forever. Though, one of us would lose our voice, and then the other would, and the conversation would be reduced to heavy breathing… Heat raced over my skin at the idea of the ways I could touch myself, to breathe heavily for him. "Says the man who ordered me to send him pussy pictures."

"An order you argued with, despite planning on doing it anyway."

"Busted." I laughed.

"I should let you get some sleep."

Oh. Such a simple, thoughtful statement, but it hurt. The pain was a good reminder that I shouldn't be flirting with him, given the business nature of our relationship. "Probably a good idea."

"One more thing, though."

This was where he'd make his pitch. Because why not end the conversation on a down note? "All right?"

"I'll be in New Orleans in a few nights, if you'd like a remote tour."

My heart body-checked my brain and slammed it out of the ring. "I'd love that."

"It's a da—eal. Sweet dreams."

"'Night." I set my phone on the nightstand.

My brain had recovered. Was this part of the pitch? Kingston told me flat out that their goal was to convince me they'd be good business partners.

The ache behind my ribs desperately wanted that call to be what it looked like on the surface—friendly and flirty. But I couldn't believe nothing hid underneath.

Chapter Thirteen

Thursday night, Kingston slipped through the café front door as I was locking up. His hair was damp, and hints of the next wave of storm dotted his shirt. He fixed me with a smile that he must think was irresistible.

He was right.

"We're not open, sir." I rarely closed shop, but that was how the schedules fell today.

He didn't look deterred. "Perfect. Then you're free to hang out. I'm taking you to dinner."

I raised my eyebrows at the assumption. "Since when?"

"Since…" He looked at his phone "I assume about two minutes from now."

"What happens in two minutes?"

"I convince you to say yes."

Arrogant bastard. I should be annoyed. The best I could summon was cautious. "Is this all part of your plan to prove to me what a good business partner you'd be?"

Kingston searched my face. "Does that get you to join me?"

"No." It would put an immediate end to the conversation. Which was best for everyone.

His grin was back. "Good, because I didn't want to lie about my intentions. I want your company for the night."

My heart did a happy skip-jump-hop at the sparkle in his dark eyes. "I don't know."

"What would it take to convince you?"

"How long is left on the clock?" Why couldn't I keep myself in check around these two?

"Let's call it *Time's Up*, for simplicity's sake." He pocketed his phone. "I promise you a night you'll never forget."

An easy guarantee, given how hard it was to get them out of my head anyway. "All right. You're on." I swore a chorus of singing forest animals broke out in my skull.

When he offered his arm this time, I nestled my hand into the crook of his elbow. Light raindrops pattered on us as we strolled down the front walk to his SUV rental. He opened the passenger door, and made sure I was seated, before hurrying to take his own seat.

Rush hour traffic was thinning, so we were on the freeway within minutes, which was when it occurred to me that we were heading toward the mountains. Park City? Did he think a fancy dinner would leave a bigger impression on me? "Where are we going? Or is it a surprise."

"Kind of, not really? My original plan was a picnic in the mountains, but since it's raining, it'll have to be an in-car one."

Damn-it-all, now I was swooning again. "I haven't been on a picnic in forever." Not a real one. For months after I bought my property, it was nightly picnics.

"No time?" Kingston asked.

Owen must have told him what we talked about last night. That made the most sense, but for some reason I didn't think that was the case. "How'd you guess?"

"I've been where you are. Where operating in the black become the single consuming goal in life."

"I thought this wasn't about a sales pitch," I teased.

"It's not. I'm making a simple observation. I'm capable of those, too." The shift in his voice was something I couldn't name.

"Never doubted it for a moment."

"How about this—If I intend to make you another business pitch, I'll warn you first."

That sounded convenient. "Like, a big flashing beacon?"

"A verbal one. Along the lines of *whoop whoop, warning. Incoming sales pitch. Whoop whoop.*"

I laughed. "I *would* appreciate the heads up."

"It's a deal then. Otherwise, anything we talk about, shop related or not, is us getting to know each other. Period."

"Why?" It was a simple question, with a complex background. I didn't understand, if he wasn't trying to win me over for business, where was all the effort coming from?

Kingston glanced at me, then steered us across three lanes of freeway to pull onto the shoulder and stop. The light traffic was a savior, but the rain was pouring down now, making it dark as night out here. This hardly seemed like a safe place to have a conversation.

He put on the emergency flashers, shifted in his seat to face me, and gripped my chin enough to hold my gaze to his. "I get the feeling you don't always listen to me."

His touch didn't hurt, but the accusation did. He commanded attention. There was a strength and intensity in his fingers that made my pulse roar.

"I hear everything you tell me," I said.

"But you're not actually listening." The power that spilled from him stole my breath. "Pay attention. You're intelligent. Funny. Gorgeous—head to toe and *every* bit in between. I'm here because I want to get to know you. Period. No qualifiers."

I couldn't grasp a response. The best I could manage was to stare back with wide eyes.

"Are we on the same page now?" he asked.

I nodded.

Kingston's grin was back. The flipped switch between serious and playful was almost as disconcerting as the way my body reacted to him. "Good." He crushed his lips to mine, and spent several seconds licking, nibbling, and dancing his tongue around mine.

I was breathless when he pulled away.

"Picnic awaits." He pulled back onto the road.

Should I be scared of the mercurial moods? I didn't get the impression he'd hurt me, or that he'd even consider it. What I did see was an alternate version of what I did. I hadn't wanted to admit such a sexy, self-assured guy could be dealing with any sort of insecurity, but he was hiding something under the humor. Not about me, but about how he wanted the world to see him versus how he thought it did.

"Tell me about you," Kingston said.

I had a practiced pitch I could give to most people when they asked this question. If Owen had asked me directly last night, he'd have gotten the same thing. "I was raised in a happy, lower middle-class family, went to private school—"

"Uniform? Plaid skirt, white shirt, knee-high socks?"

"Khaki's and polo shirts."

"Don't destroy the fantasy." Yup, playful Kingston was back. "That image is going in its own folder in my brain."

"I own one. A short plaid skirt." Why did I say that? Because I loved this attention, duh.

He licked his lips. "Even better. Sorry to interrupt, fantasy saved, please continue."

I'd been thrown out of the rhythm of my story. "Umm… dance in high school"—I almost stalled on the memory, thanks to my derailed train of thought, but I bit back the negative association—"community college, Associate's in business, office manager work while I saved my pennies, and then I found a cheap house up for auction, which brings us to here."

"I feel like there are some pieces missing in that story."

"I could say the same to you." I meant as far as his tale about how they'd bought their first shop.

"You *were* listening."

Of course. Listening and my self-doubt clashed, but I heard what he said. "I told you so."

"So I caught up on *Spring Popcorn*. There are absolutely no dragons or Nazi's," he said.

I was grateful he didn't press my omission of information. "No? Maybe I read a different version."

asking for it

"The one in your head?" His tone was teasingly accusatory.

"Exactly."

We slid from *Spring Popcorn* to other manga and comics, our favorite TV shows and books… It was easy to talk to him. I suspected as much, based on our previous conversations, but there was some doubt with us talking one-on-one. I liked that we had so much in common, and that what we didn't wasn't an obstacle.

He drove us into Big Cottonwood Canyon, navigating the roads with practiced ease. He wasn't intimidated by mountain driving.

We parked a way back from the main roads, in a wooded clearing. The scents of dirt, pine trees, rain, and the faint hint of Kingston's cologne were borderline arousing.

He shut off the engine. "I may not have thought this through one-hundred percent."

"Oh?"

"My plan was that we'd eat in the back of the SUV, but we still have to get back there."

"I don't mind getting a little wet." Why didn't I realize how that sounded *before* I said it?

"So I've seen."

I shook my head, but couldn't hide my amusement. "Wet in the rain. See?" I opened the door and stepped out.

The rain was coming down a lot harder than I expected, and my shriek ended in a giggle when I was soaked within seconds.

"You're right, wet is good." Kingston was by my side.

From his gravely tone, I expected to find him staring at my chest, but his gaze was fixed on my face. Raindrops pelted me. My hair clung to my cheeks. None of it mattered, because I couldn't turn away from the way he watched me.

No one had ever looked at me like that before. Like I was the only person he could see. Like I was his sole focus.

Kingston brushed his hair off my face, and his mouth over mine. His kiss seared my soul. I almost expected to see the rain evaporate before it hit us. It was just a kiss, but it tingled through all of me.

I whimpered when he broke the sweet, intense kiss. He pressed his forehead to mine. "Dinner?"

"Isn't that what we're doing out here?" My half-joke came out breathless.

"You're more like dessert, but we can have that first, if you want to be stripped down—"

"No." My response came down more forcefully than I intended, propelled by the chill that raced down my spine. Hello, unwelcome and traumatic memory. "That is… Not out here."

asking for it

He tangled his fingers with mine. "Okay. Dinner."

I was grateful he didn't ask *why*? I couldn't relive that moment enough to talk about it. It already haunted my dreams too often.

Chapter Fourteen

Kingston raised the rear door as a temporary shelter from the rain. There was already a blanket unfurled in the back of the SUV.

"We'll get your blanket all wet," I said.

"The blanket can be washed." He moved the quilt to the edge of the SUV, so we could sit with our legs hanging outside, then grabbed a cooler from where it was secured near the seats, and pulled it forward as well.

Kingston extracted a tray of fresh fruit and cheese. It looked delicious.

Which must be why the nagging in my head asked *Does he think I need more fruit?* Now that the edges of old wounds had been exposed, my insecurities could rush back. I tried to argue with myself that fruit was all I ate at the cabin, and I made a fuss about the salad the first day I met the guys.

"Why fruit?" I forced out the neutral question.

He plucked a large strawberry from the mix, and traced it along my bottom lip, drawing a gasp from me.

asking for it

"Take a bite," he said.

I did. There was really no dainty way to bite into a strawberry so big, and juice dribbled down my chin.

Kingston leaned in and dragged his tongue up, licking the mess away. "That's why," he murmured against my lips.

He was toeing into dangerously perfect territory. Making it difficult to remember if I had reservations about liking him. Lulling me into security.

"I won't look nearly as sexy eating cheese." I needed to lighten the mood.

"All a matter of opinion."

I held a cheese cube up in the air. "Really?"

He drew my fingers and the food into his mouth, licking along the pads of my skin, before pulling away, taking my breath with him.

"Let's just say the chocolate frosting event left an impression on me." He brushed his lips over mine. "Laying you out and eating dinner off you may have become a favorite fantasy."

I couldn't… but my imagination said I certainly could let him do something like that, just not out in the open. I squeezed my thighs together, but it didn't suppress the throb. "Something to try later."

"I was hoping you'd say that."

I didn't know how to follow a line of conversation like that, so I stuffed a few grapes into my mouth.

"You're no stranger to the picnic lifestyle." Kingston joined me in eating.

"When I first bought my property, I did a lot of blanket-on-the-floor meals."

He tilted his head and studied me. "I'm intrigued."

"It's not a super fascinating story. I bought the house in auction, and I was certain I had enough left over for the renovations. I'm smart, I could figure out how to do the work myself, with videos and such." I laughed at past me's naiveté. "I was so very wrong."

Kingston shook his head. "Yeah, a lot of that stuff isn't really a one-person job."

"Especially if you don't know what you're doing." I could admit that. Now. "So I was putting all of my money into sheetrock, tile, and appliances, rather than furniture, but I couldn't install any of it."

"You obviously figured something out."

I got lucky. That was all there was to it. "I was at the fabric store, torn over upholstery, and this cute pink-haired girl introduced herself." Sadie basically adopted me.

"Ah, the extrovert swoops in and makes themselves at home in the introvert's life. I love that kind of story."

asking for it

I didn't have to ask which he was. "I don't suppose you have a similar tale about Owen."

"There was math involved, rather than fabric, but finish your story first."

Math. I was definitely curious. "One of her friends came from a family of contractors, and he knew how to do a lot of what I needed. She got them to provide the manual labor, a few of them installed my network, and we pulled everything together into Phase One of Loading Java. I still went way over budget. I slept on an air mattress, with none of my own real furniture, for a long time. A couple of them even worked for me for free until I could afford employees." I owed Sadie a lot. And Grayson. And Anne, Jax, Chase…

"Your friends are good people."

Fewer things were more true. "They are. You'd like them."

"I look forward to meeting them."

Were we at a *introduce me to your friends* point in our relationship? Since I'd already met his, it seemed so.

We talked some more, put away the food, and kept talking. I lost track of time as the rain slowed to a drizzle.

A gust of wind tore through the night, and I shivered at the sudden chill.

"You could always strip out of those wet clothes," Kingston said.

The casual suggestion didn't hit me as hard as before, but I still wasn't up for any nudity outside of my own home. "I'm fine."

He crawled back into the SUV, and grabbed something from the back seat. "Come here." He crooked his finger.

I joined him, and sat next to him when he patted the vehicle. He wrapped us both in a fresh blanket.

"Better?" he asked.

Warm. Safe. Comfortable. Pressed against him? It was pretty much heaven. "Better."

Silence settled between us. It was as comfortable as leaning against him. How screwed was I, that I wanted to make a habit of picnics in the rain with Kingston?

"We almost lost our first shop, too." His voice was subdued.

"What happened?"

He sighed. "My mother was upset that I'd invested in such a piece of shit idea. She cut me off. Disowned me." The pain in his voice was like a knife through the heart.

"I'm sorry."

He shook his head. "It's okay. I mean, it's not, but… what are you going to do, right? Anyway, we were out of cash, and we were determined to make the thing take off. Every cent we made from the shop went back into it. We'd work the café all day, and then go to second jobs at night. Owen was cooking, and I was washing dishes. Working at a restaurant had the added bonus of free food. No air mattress, but we did have a shitty motel room with only one bed."

"Wow." I wanted to say I couldn't imagine, but I had a pretty good idea. I hadn't been close to starving, but it was rough in the beginning. "You spun it into something big, though."

"We did. And there's a lot of satisfaction in that."

I wanted to ask if he ever repaired things with his mother, but was that appropriate when a relationship ended that way?

"I still don't talk to her," he said, as if reading my mind. "It doesn't matter what we've done with the place, to her it's still not a proper way to earn a living. When I figured out nothing I did would be good enough, I severed ties."

"I'm sorry. I wish I had something better to say."

Kingston kissed me on the forehead. "You mean it, and that's what matters."

As we settled into silence again, drowsiness pulled my eyelids shut. I struggled to pry them open again.

"Hey." Kingston shook me gently. "Come on. I'll take you home."

Embarrassment coursed through me. "I promise it's not you." Or rather, it was, but not in the way falling asleep on a date looked. I was letting my guard down around him.

"How much sleep do you get at night?"

"Enough." Four to six hours.

He climbed from the SUV and helped me do the same. "Not enough," he argued. "But I'm flattered you trust me enough to sleep here."

I did. That should be a scary thought. It wasn't, though.

He kept an arm around my waist as he walked me to the front of the vehicle, and made sure I was settled inside.

I didn't mean to doze on the way home, but the next thing I knew, we were parked behind my house.

"I'm a lousy date." My voice was gravelly from being woken up. "Falling asleep on you over and over."

"You're the best date I've ever had."

When he said things like that, my insides melted. "I'm not so tired I won't remember that in the morning." Did that make sense? I wasn't sure.

"Good." He brushed his lips over mine. "Thank you for tonight."

asking for it

He waited until I was inside, and then drove away.

I leaned against the back door, and stared at the ceiling. I wanted more. Another night with him. Another kiss. Another fuck. Another anything.

At the same time, that sales pitch was still looming. It didn't matter that Kingston wanted to get to know me, or that Owen had called just to talk… It didn't change their ultimate goal, and it didn't change that I'd pick my business over anything in this world except my friends.

There was a looming expiration date on Kingston and Owen's being in my life. There was no other way to look at things.

Chapter Fifteen

My next couple of days were disrupted by fantasy enhanced memories of Kingston, especially any time I was in the kitchen.

My dreams were mostly of Owen whispering in my ear in that deep, seductive tone. He wasn't always saying sexy things, sometimes it was as simple as *Willis Tower lights up at night, and it's the most amazing display of technology meets art.*

When Owen called me on Saturday night, anticipation tightened in my belly just from seeing his name on the screen.

"Hey, Kitty Cat." His voice and the nickname caressed my senses.

Were aural orgasms a thing? I was starting to think so. "Hey, yourself. We've moved on to pet names now?"

"Pet, Kitty Cat, I get it." He chuckled. "You ever send anyone else a picture of your fleecy pussy?"

"Never once."

asking for it

"Then you're only *Kitty Cat* to me. I like the exclusivity of that." He was starting off strong.

Not that I minded. Maybe I should. But it felt amazing to just hear him, that he'd called, that this was so easy to slide into... I couldn't take issue with any of it. "You're definitely a club of one."

"Question for you. Where have you always wanted to visit?"

"Tokyo." I didn't need to think about my answer. "I want to see a real cosplay café, and wander a city that's amazingly huge on the inside, but still has a connection to nature farther out. Don't suppose that's on your list of places you'd set up a shop." Why would I ask that? Because Even though I'd barely known them more than a week, I was reaching a point where I couldn't picture them not in my life.

Owen's laugh was light. "It's on my to-visit list. Not sure I want to consider the cost of doing international business, or of property there, but I'd definitely take a vacation or three."

"Take lots of pictures." I pushed out the casual words instead of the *make sure you take me* that wanted to force its way out. "How's New Orleans?" Best to change the subject now, before I said something I couldn't take back.

"I have a confession to make."

I didn't call to give you a tour. The flirting is just to loosen you up for business.

It was easier to ignore my doubts than I expected. "I'm listening."

"I don't ever do touristy things when I travel for business," Owen said. "But I wanted to give you more than just a description of the view from my hotel, especially since I'm facing a brick wall, so last night I agreed to go on a ghost tour with the couple who manages the shop here."

"You did that *just* for me?" I was flattered, and only a little skeptical.

"Absolutely."

"You didn't enjoy it at all."

"It was ludicrous. Superstition, hokey myths... Fuck. You don't believe, do you?"

I was amused by his sudden concern. "I'm not sure. Maybe, maybe not. But that doesn't answer my question. Did you enjoy it?"

"Technically you didn't ask a question. But yes, it was entertaining as hell."

I settled onto my bed, back against the headboard and pillow in my lap. "Tell me about it."

I listened as he described the buildings, the legends, and some of the ghosts who were said to haunt the various stops they made. He gave vivid details of the architecture and folklore, but seemed to have an instinct for not lingering too long on any one thing.

I was captivated. Though honestly, I probably would have been captivated if he'd read me a croissant recipe.

"And there was a tarot reader at the end of the tour. I had to pick a card, of course," he said.

I grinned. "Of course." I'd always been fascinated by tarot cards and fortune telling. Luna could read them, and she'd had me pick a card a few times, but I was firmly in the *it may or may not be real* camp. "What card did you get? What does your future hold?"

"Three of swords," Owen said. "Apparently it has something to do with romantic betrayal."

As in, I'd betray him? A shiver ran through me, and I hugged the pillow. "That's haunting."

"Good thing I don't believe." Owen sounded unfazed. "Fuck. Don't tell Kingston I'm talking shit about this stuff."

Curious. Not enough to wipe the tarot reading from my mind, but a good distraction. "Okay, one, why not, and two what makes you think I'm talking to Kingston?"

"Because he told me. And because he *does* believe."

Somehow I wasn't surprised that they held such a deep-seated belief in opposition, but were friends in spite of it. "The two of you are close." *Duh.* But were Owen and I close enough he'd give me more of an answer than before about his relationship with Kingston?

"I love him." Owen said the words with all the assurance of a man who wasn't terrified of being called less-than-masculine. So, so sexy.

But did he mean the same thing I heard? "When you say *love*, is this a romantic thing or more familial? Have you told Kingston? Because what the two of you have is a little more than *occasional benefits*."

Owen sighed. "That's a lot to answer at once."

"And best done with emotion, not logic," I teased.

"Ouch."

"Another emotion. Good job." I made sure my tone conveyed playfulness rather than trying to shut him down.

Owen chuckled dryly. "Yeah, the two of you bring that out in me. But… I don't have the kinds of answers I think you want. I love him. I'd do most anything for him. I've never specifically used those words with him."

"Maybe tell him, instead of making excuses to be with him through a third party?" Given I had been—was still?—that third party, was I talking myself out of… something more? Of all the things I

asking for it

was worried about when it came to them, that wasn't on the list.

"I don't make excuses," Owen said. "If I want sex, I ask for sex."

So I'd seen. The heat of memory flushed my skin. "Sex, yes. You're very skilled at sex and asking for it. I meant the rest."

Another sigh. "This is going to sound melodramatic, but Kingston and I saved each other."

Interesting detour, but I didn't mind. Each glimpse into their pasts made them more real. More desirable. If I asked for details, I'd be another step closer to having to admit they were more than just casual fun. "How'd you meet?"

"Math."

The same thing Kingston said. It was nice to know their single word stories matched up.

"Is there more to it than that? Is this a *Math Saves* kind of public safety warning?" I teased.

His breathing shifted for a heartbeat, a heavier puff. I pictured him on the other end of the line huffing out dry amusement. "His parents paid me to tutor him in math when we were in junior high. Except he didn't need it. He wasn't actually failing, but anything less than an *A* was disgraceful to them, and he understood it, he was just bored, and didn't want excelling to damage his *I don't give a fuck* reputation."

A young Kingston putting more effort into what people thought than a mark on a paper? Easy to believe.

"I was the brooding smart kid no one wanted to approach back then," Owen said.

"I know that feeling." I'd been a lot the same. *Resting bitch everything.*

"But Kingston looked past that. He sort of... adopted me."

The extrovert bringing the introvert into their fold.

"He brought his grades up," Owen continued. "To prove I was doing what his parents wanted, and so they'd keep paying me." A pause. It ticked on longer than a breath or two "It was what we both needed at the time. He's a good guy and he deserves good things."

I didn't know how to interpret that. "It feels like you're directing that at me."

Another pause.

It would be nice if I could say Owen's hesitations didn't mean anything, but he was measuring his words. Each time the silence drifted in like this.

"I am." He finally spoke. "He and I... What we have works. You're a good thing, Kitty Cat. Amazing, in fact."

asking for it

Now I was the one who had to consider my next words. Instinct wanted to say *no I'm not.* Few people reacted well to a compliment shut down like that, but especially these two. "Thank you?"

"I'm glad the two of you are hanging out. I should let you go before it gets too late. Sweet dreams."

The abrupt wrap-up ground through me, stealing any questions I had. "You too."

I disconnected, but sleep wouldn't be my friend tonight. I was too caught up in analyzing the intricacies of the conversation with Owen.

Chapter Sixteen

My phone chimed early in the morning. I'd think it was Anne, but it was the default tone, not our custom one.

You up? The name on the screen said *Persistent Asshole*.

The label I'd given him when he was calling every few weeks trying to buy my business. I should update that to have his real name. *Depends on who this is ;)*

My phone rang seconds after I hit *Send*.

"Your concierge and tour guide for the day," Kingston said the instant I answered.

Maybe I wouldn't change the name on his contact, though I might add a smiley face at the end. "What if I have other plans?"

"Cancel them. What I have for you is a million times better."

"Which is...?"

"A surprise."

Nope. "I don't do surprises."

asking for it

"Oh." He managed to encompass *deflated* in a single syllable. "In that case, I have a friend in management at Digital Media, and he's screening their new game for a few people."

It wasn't strawberries in the rain, and it was *fraternizing with the enemy*. But it did sound fun. Besides, I wanted to see him and I wasn't actually doing anything else. "Is it any sort of conflict of interest that some of my closest friends work for the competition?"

"Was it when you catered for DM?"

No. "I take a non-disclosure agreement seriously."

"Then it's not a problem now. I'll pick you up in thirty minutes, and we'll get breakfast first." He made the decision sound so simple.

But wasn't it?

Thirty minutes was both way too much time, since I was already up and dressed for the day, and not nearly enough to sift through my entire closet for a different outfit that looked sexy-cute without looking like I was trying too hard.

A skirt was tempting, especially the plaid one hanging in the back, but not in front of other people. Especially not people I did business with.

I settled on a sun dress that flared out under my breasts, and a crop sweater. Mickey Mouse ears decorated the dress—I would be the perfect blend of playful and professional.

My doorbell chiming saved me from second-guessing the decision. I grabbed my purse and phone, and headed downstairs to answer.

When I opened the door, Kingston whistled. "My memory always understates how gorgeous you are," he said.

"Thank you." I'd need to practice accepting praise, if they were going to keep showering me with it. When did I make the shift from questioning everything kind they said to believing they meant it? Was I letting my guard down too quickly?

As we drove to breakfast, my phone chimed again. *That* was one of my friends. "I should turn this off," I muttered, swiping at the screen.

"I don't want you to miss anything important."

And I wasn't up for talking to Sadie in front of Kingston. "It's a friend. I'll call her back."

"I don't mind."

"I don't want them to know I'm with you." Why did I say that? I could have gone with *really, it'll wait*. But I had to be honest instead.

Kingston's expression shifted to disconcertingly neutral. "Why not?"

Because they looked out for me. That I was out with *him* might not be easy to understand. I didn't want my friends to judge me. Not that they ever had, but they'd never seen me do something like this. "Last time I told them about you, you were the asshole who wanted buy my shop, and slept with me to get to it."

"Except I didn't, and they're not going to know otherwise until you tell them." He was frowning now. It was better than no emotion, but it still hurt to see.

"I'm sorry. You've been honest with me from the start—except that whole fake name thing—this is all coming out wrong."

His frown relaxed. "Happens to the best of us."

"If you're sure you don't mind..."

"You telling your friends I'm not actually an asshole? I'm pretty sure." Now the teasing was back.

Telling Sadie meant admitting this was more than a fling, but not saying anything hurt Kingston. I didn't want to do that, because I cared that he was happy. Maybe this *was* more than a fling. A fling with a guy whose best friend loved him. With said best friend apparently trying to push us together. How did this get so complicated so quickly?

I called Sadie back.

"Hey." She was cheerful. "Stopped by your place and you were gone. Are you busy today?"

"You know it's ungodly early on a Sunday, right?" I teased. Anything before ten was a foul thought to Sadie.

"I'm aware." Her huff was playful. "But last week you seemed sad, and I haven't heard from you since, so I'm checking in with you."

The concern warmed me. "I'm good." Her bringing up last week was the perfect segue to where I was, but more stuck in my throat.

Kingston rested his hand on my knee, sending a shower of sparks to mingle with my hesitation.

"Are you sure? Do you want to hang out? I miss you," Sadie said.

I did adore her. "I'm... rain check? I'm on a date."

"Is that code for *I woke up in a stranger's bed and I don't know how to get out of here without a fuss. Save me*? Say *yes* and I've got your back."

Because I didn't date. "No. An actual date."

Kingston pulled into the parking lot of a diner, and shut off the engine.

"Is that why you're not calling us?" Excitement bled into Sadie's voice. "Tell me all about him. No, wait, you're with him now. Tell him you need friend approval. Not that you do, but I want to see this guy that Lyn is willing to call a *date*. Do you like him? Of course you do. How did you meet him?"

She didn't expect me to answer all of her questions, but the last one was the most important. I glanced at Kingston, who was watching me, then tried to force my thoughts into some semblance of order. "You know how I told you about those guys who want to buy my shop?"

"And the sex? And the assho— oh, no. Lyn."

Was that disappointment? Judgment? "Yes." I switched the phone over to FaceTime. Sadie wouldn't filter herself and I needed that right now. I showed her Kingston.

He grinned and waved. "Kingston. Asshole Extraordinaire, at your service... Holy shit, you're *Sadie Sews*."

"Not relevant. What did you do to my Lyn?" Sadie demanded.

"Well... I screwed up, I begged for her forgiveness, and then I begged again to spend more time with her. Do you have any idea how amazing your friend is?"

Sadie shook her head. "Better than you do."

"Fair point, though I'd like to move up a little farther on the scale."

It was odd to hear me talked about this way. A girl could get used to the indirect praise.

"He's cute." Sadie was talking to me again. "Does he know if he hurts you, there's no place in the world he can hide from us?"

"He does now, and he would deserve it," Kingston said.

Grayson walked behind Sadie, then paused. "Who's the hottie?" He asked.

Sadie gleaned back. "Lyn's new manservant."

Sadie, Anne, and I teased each other and their boyfriends all the time, but that was inner circle stuff. Did I want them drawing Kingston into the same?

"Ready to serve at Her Majesty's whim." He fell into it so easily.

What if he fit in with us? What if Owen did? They'd have to, for me to stay with them. Was I thinking about long term with them? No. I was living this day today. "Anyway," I said. "He made nice, we're good now, and he asked first if I was free. I'll call you tomorrow and we'll figure something out?"

"Yes. Definitely yes." Sadie was emphatic. "You have so much to fill me in on."

And with any luck, I'd figure out at least some of it before we spoke again.

"That went well. It seemed to go well." Kingston tangled his fingers with mine as we headed inside. "You tell me. Did that go well?"

"She didn't threaten to send the cops, so..."

"Good thing I never plan on hurting you."

Except for that whole looming matter of him and Owen wanting to buy my shop. And Owen being in love with him... Did Kingston feel the same? Would he if he knew? *Did* he know?

Gah. Too many questions, and I just wanted to hang out and have fun.

asking for it

We were seated, and ordered coffee. As soon as the waitress left, Kingston leaned in. "I can't believe Sadie and Grayson know you."

"Grayson did half the wiring in Loading Java." I wasn't surprised he knew who they were. Sadie had a huge online following with her costume design, and Grayson was a popular game streamer. Even if Kingston only followed one of them, they frequently appeared on each other's channels.

Kingston tapped his index finger on the table rapidly. Odd twitch. He huffed out a breath. "I heard… The two of them… Is it true?"

"Is what true?"

"She's married to him and his boyfriend."

It had been a gorgeous ceremony. Held in my back yard. "It's true."

Kingston shook his head.

"What?" I asked.

"Nothing. Or rather, I'm processing. In a good way."

I wasn't going to read into that.

Ha, I totally was. I could make so many assumptions regarding why Kingston cared if Sadie was married to two people. The obvious one for most people would focus on my relationship with him and Owen. But my brain revolted at the thought. Not because I didn't like it, but because it was so implausible.

Wasn't it?

I stashed the familiar insecurities about me being undesirable, and dove into the now instead. Breakfast—the conversation and attention that went with it—was fun. So was the unofficial demo with Kingston's friend from DM. I even got my name on the demo copy list, to give me promo for my shop.

By the end of the day, I wasn't thinking about anything but how much I enjoyed spending time with Kingston.

He walked me to the back door at my place.

"Do you want to come in?" I had things to do before tomorrow, but I didn't want to give him up just yet.

He brushed his lips over mine in the most agonizingly sweet kiss. "Desperately."

I unlocked the door.

"But I won't," Kingston said.

My heart ground to a halt, slamming into my ribs with a painful *crunch*. I couldn't hide my frown.

"If I come in, I'm going to want to kiss you. And undress you. And kiss you some more, until you're writing in pleasure and your legs are too weak to stand."

Me too. "Is that bad?"

He shook his head. "I don't want sex to define whatever happens next."

asking for it

"That's sweet." Disappointing, but also reasonable.

"I was hoping for *noble* but I'll take *sweet*. I'll still leave you with something, though." He wrapped one arm around my waist, gripped the back of my neck, and crushed his mouth to mine.

My body molded to his hard frame. Everywhere we made contact, despite there being layers of clothing between us, my skin scorched with need. His erection dug into my stomach. Desire throbbed between my thighs. This felt so… *real*.

Kingston broke away with a groan. He dragged a thumb over my lips. "I'm going to be gone for a few days, fetching some things from my old place. I'll call you as soon as I know when I'll be back."

"I don't drop everything for just anyone." Did that sound light? Carefree?

"I'm special."

He really was.

I nodded. "I'll talk to you then."

He brushed his lips over mine again. "Don't forget about me while I'm gone."

"I'll try not to." Not that I ever could. Whatever happened, Kingston was a permanent part of my memories.

Chapter Seventeen

Sadie and Anne were supportive and happy for me when I gave them more details about what I'd been up to with Owen and Kingston. I shouldn't have expected otherwise, but my self-esteem was a massive bitch whenever she felt tiny.

Weeks passed, and summer melted into not-quite-summer at an agonizingly slow rate. My days went the same as always, with me getting up early to bake for the shop, and working all day. But my nights were marked by if I got to talk to Owen, or go out with Kingston. When neither was available, I went to bed early and let pleasant dreams of either or both men keep me company.

It didn't matter that Owen and I limited our conversations to *friendly* topics rather than *romantic*, or that my dates with Kingston never ended with more than a kiss. I'd never felt so adored. I'd never enjoyed anyone's company so much outside of Anne and Sadie.

One Friday night, a little more than a month after I first met them, I was talking to Owen. I'd hesitated to bring up *Kingston* and *love* again, on the off chance it put an end to these conversations. Apparently I was a little worried after all.

Owen was on the last leg of his trip, and had already described several parts of Atlanta for me. The conversation drifted where it would, and I wasn't in a hurry to hang up, even though I had to be up early. I wanted to know why, out of all the degrees Owen could have pursued with his knowledge and interests, he chose a cooking.

"I love too cook." He made it sound so simple. "And I wanted to go into the restaurant business. For me, school was one of my steps. Why an anime gaming café? The real reason, not the flippant answer you gave Ravyn and Ramsey."

I wasn't willing to admit this to many people, but it felt okay to tell Owen. "It combines my three favorite things… Anime, gaming, and food, in case that wasn't clear."

I could have guessed you love food. My insecurity spoke in his voice. But those scars were far older than he was, and he didn't deserve to fall under their scrutiny.

"It's scary how much we have in common," he said.

"I know what you mean."

"Have you got your pussy on display tonight?" Owen's tone was playful.

I smiled at the memory. "No, but I am laying here in nothing but panties and a camisole."

If he said *show me,* I didn't know what I'd do. There were some things I wasn't willing to commit to photo.

Silence.

What was he considering?

"Tonight, I want the guided tour." His voice had dropped an octave. "Put me on speaker, lay back, run your hands over your body, and tell me how every single bit of it feels."

I set my phone aside. I'd never done anything like this before, but for him, I wanted to, and I wanted the moment to be perfect. "Where should I start?" I couldn't hide the quiver in my voice.

"Over your top, your breasts. I want to hear your gasps as you tease yourself through the fabric."

I glided my hands up my torso, the way he told me to, moaning when I brushed over the more erogenous bits.

"Fuck." Owen's voice an octave lower was even better. "Are your nipples hard? Tell me how it feels."

Hesitation lodged my reply in my throat, but the compulsion to please Owen won out. I teased the nubs, my shirt rubbing against them and adding extra friction. "They rock hard. It feels so good."

asking for it

Good enough I kept playing. Moaning. Not trying to bite back any noises that wanted to slip from my throat.

"Top off," Owen said.

I stripped off my cami. "Done."

"I wish I was there. I can picture your gorgeous breasts. Pale skin. Delicious nipples. What it's like to draw one into my mouth, and suck until you whimper."

Memory mingled with now. "I'm licking one." I pressed my breast up and flicked my tongue out. "And pinching." Being in the moment made it easier to describe things. I rolled a nipple between my fingers, gasping with each touch. "It's not as good as your mouth, though."

Owen grunted. "God, I can almost taste you. I'm so hard right now. Keep playing, Kitty Cat."

I did—twisting and rolling—how long did he want me to do this for? It felt good, but it wasn't enough. "I'm squeezing my thighs together." My confession came out breathy. "I want more."

His guttural, "Hmm…" rolled over me. "Slide your fingers between your legs. Tell me what it feels like."

It felt like I wanted him here, those solid arms pinning my hands above my head while he pounded inside me. "I'm wet. Slippery. My panties are… useless."

"Take them off. I want you naked in bed, thinking about me."

"Done."

Owen's chuckle was gravel. "Spread your legs. Imagine me kneeling between them."

"Like I could think of anything else right now."

"There are so many nights I wish you and I had…" Owen trailed into one of those pauses. Instead of making me nervous, it built the anticipation, because I wished the same. "I'm stroking my cock," he said. "Imagining sliding inside you. You're so fucking tight. Slick. Perfect."

"I'm using my fingers." I pushed three inside myself. "It's good, but not the same."

"No toys?"

I had plenty, but they would stay in the drawer for now. "It's not the same. I want to get lost in the fantasy of skin on skin."

"*Christ*. Me too. Make yourself come, Kitty Cat. I want to hear the incredible sounds you make."

Usually when I masturbated, I didn't have the patience to hold out. But if I lasted longer, I kept Owen on the phone longer. I slipped between teasing my clit and dipping my fingers inside me. I lost track of talking and myself in the sensations, and letting them tear noises from me.

I held out as long as I could, but I hovered on the edge of orgasm, and had to push myself over.

When I came, I let the cries and moans fall into the room, until my throat was dry and I was spent.

"Fucking hell, gorgeous." Owen grunted as much as spoke. "I'm fisting my cock and stroking so hard it aches."

I relaxed back into the sheets, and listened to his noises. Boldness, carried on post-orgasm bliss, filled me. "If you were here, I'd wrap my lips around you, then beg you to come inside me."

"*Jesus*." The noises Owen made were guttural. Almost primal. His breathing grew stuttered, followed by a rapid series of grunts, and one long one.

And then silence.

"You still there?" he asked roughly.

"Yes."

"I wish you were here instead."

I physically felt that sentiment. "Me too."

"You're incredible."

I didn't know how to respond. Another compliment, and I didn't want to ruin the warm fuzzy glow. "How did you know?" My question was breathy.

"Know what? That you're incredible? It's pretty obvious."

Thankfully no one could see how bright red I must be, flushed from the string of kind words. How to phrase my question? "You didn't ask for pictures this time."

"You don't like pictures of yourself."

"That's true…"

"Don't misunderstand"—Owen's voice was throaty, rasping over me—"I love that photo of Kitty Cat Lyn. But I don't want to push you away. Never, but especially tonight." Did his voice catch?

"When *will* you be here? I want to actually feel you next time," I said.

Empty air.

No. Nonononono.

"I fucked up." Owen's regret sent fissures of doubt through me.

My blood curdled. I wouldn't jump to conclusions, no matter how loudly my brain was screaming that this was it. This was when the betrayal happened. "Not what a girl wants to hear after sex, even the long-distance kind."

"I want to be there. Have you here. Something that lets me touch you. But…" His sigh opened the chasm of doubt wider. "Kingston likes you. Adores you. I— I should let him tell you that but it's context. I told you I'd do anything for him."

I didn't know how to react. My thoughts were split between terror of this being a charade and fear of it being more. Being what my heart hoped for. "Okay?"

asking for it

"I was supposed to keep my distance. Be the good, supportive friend. His wingman. Let things go where they would with him and you." The husky, deep sound of Owen's voice, the one that sent goosebumps racing over me, was back. "And instead I'm falling for you. I don't want to take you away from him. I want you both—wow, that sounds even better aloud than in my head."

My heart plummeted into my shoes. *I want all of that too*, the words jammed in my throat. The lack of response that came out instead had to be the worst thing I could have done... aside from maybe laughing.

Owen bit off a dry chuckle. "Do you know how many logic holes exist in this relationship?"

"This isn't a relationship." I cringed at the words. Nope, that was worse than keeping my mouth shut.

"First of all, ouch. Second, anyone you interact with on any sort of ongoing basis is a relationship. You're making an assumption."

Not so much, given what he'd just confessed. "Logic holes?"

"Well, I was going to tell you three people don't stay together long term, but since you don't see what we have as *that*, there's no point." He didn't sound bitter, but his hurt was piercing.

"I had an almost identical conversation with one of my best friends before she married her boyfriends. Plural." I shouldn't be presenting counterpoints, not after the way I basically shut him down, but my heart was racing ahead of me, asking *what if?* What if things did last with them? What if everything either of them said was sincere. What if we could have warm fuzzies and fun sex and incredible conversations all the time, forever?

"I bet the three of them trust each other."

"Implicitly."

Owen sighed. "Let me rephrase my statement. Three people don't stay together long term when they don't trust each other."

I do trust you. Except when this conversation started, I'd been waiting for the other shoe to drop. Expecting this would be the end of *us*.

"You're not going to deny it," Owen said.

If only I honestly could. "If I lie and tell you *Of course I trust you*, that doesn't help the situation."

"I see."

"But I want to." That was easy to say. Out of all my stalled answers, this one was as direct and real as I got.

"Yeah?" His sadness faded. "What's it going to take to turn that into *I do*?"

Was his phrasing on purpose? Almost always. "You're doing everything right." Easier to admit than I expected. My past said they were full of shit. That there was something they were hiding from me, and it was going to destroy me. But that wasn't based on them. I might not like some of the things they'd approached me with when we met, but as far as I knew, they'd been honest since. "I guess... time. I need time, and that's on me, not you."

"I'm willing to keep going and see what happens next if you are. Kingston will be too."

Terrifying thought. Letting them into my life more than ever before. This was risk versus reward, and they were an incredible reward. "I am."

Chapter Eighteen

Every few months, we did a Cosplay Saturday theme in the café. The staff wore costumes, and we encouraged the customers to do the same.

It was a huge business day, especially since a few of our staff liked school uniforms—the men and the women—and fans would come just for the sexy-cuteness of those outfits. People would also stop by to see the spectacle, then end up staying for coffee, sweets, and sometimes gaming time.

I never dressed up. I played the *I'm the boss, I don't have to* card.

But today, I felt good. There were a lot of days like recently, but after talking to Owen last night, I was light as air.

I finished the morning's baking, including the extra for anticipated business, then headed upstairs to change. I pulled the plaid skirt from the back of my closet, paired it with black Mary Janes, white knee-highs, and a button-down white shirt. The finishing touch was twin braids.

asking for it

As I descended the back stairs, Anne's, "Holy hotness, gorgeous," greeted me.

"Hey, you made it." I skipped down the last few steps to greet her. *Damn* I felt good.

Anne gave me a noisy kiss on the cheek. "Glad I didn't miss it."

I stepped back to look her over. "Someone's out of costume."

"No, I'm not." She put her arms out and twirled. "I'm inconspicuous extra number seventy-two."

"Very specific. Why not sixty-nine?"

Anne snorted. "Because once you realize the flaws with actually doing that, the joke isn't as funny."

"You didn't think of it."

She grinned. "I didn't think of it. Forget the skirt, I love this mood on you. These guys are really good for you. When do I get to meet them?"

Heat flooded my cheeks thinking about them. "They really are incredible. Owen will be back soon."

"So… give you two weeks straight of fucking, and you might be able to make time for me?" Anne teased.

"It's not…" *that kind of relationship*. But last night it became that with Owen, and while Kingston and I hadn't slept together again, we were pushing the boundaries of what could be called *no sex*. A

159

teensy bit of me said I should be concerned about that, but I believed him when he told me why he was holding back. "I'm sure we'll need a break long before two weeks is up, to eat and stuff."

"Uh-huh."

Anne stuck around to help with the day's rush. Our other friends filtered in and out as they were able. The event was a bigger success than we'd ever had. A few more of these, and I wouldn't be worrying so much about paying the bills.

My friends took off as the crowds dwindled. My staff and I were in the process of gently shooing people out the door when a pair of arms wrapped around my waist.

"I never would have skipped class if you'd been there," Kingston murmured, before nibbling on my earlobe.

I leaned back into him. This felt so good. So right. "You skipped class? You scoundrel."

"Scoundrel? I do say, m'lady, I'm a scoundrel of the worst sort." His accent was bad enough, I couldn't identify it.

"What sort is that?"

"The sort who's hopelessly smitten."

My breath caught.

"Can your staff finish without you? We need to talk." Kingston's question was a blanket over my warm fuzzies.

Now my voice was gone for a different reason. I nodded toward the kitchen. He took my hand and led me into the other room.

I spun to face him as soon as we were through the doorway. "What's up?" I struggled to keep my tone light.

"We have a problem."

Was this it? I'd all but stopped waiting for the other shoe to drop, but I knew they still wanted this place. It was probably even more attractive after a day like today, and Kingston had promised me a warning before he pitched me again. The thought was there, but I struggled to believe it. "What kind of problem?"

"I talked to Owen this morning," he said. "I adore you so much, and I wasn't sure what to think when he brought you up."

Adore—the same word Owen used. I was pretty sure that was on a similar level as *love*, but I didn't dare read anything into this. "Do you talk about me a lot?"

"Yes. But he never tells me anything private you've told him, and I'm the same."

"So, what *are* you talking about?" This conversation wasn't going the way I expected. It could still fall apart, though.

"We talk about how incredible you are."

I smiled in spite of myself.

"And that's the problem," Kingston said. "I'm not letting you go without a fight, and neither is he."

But Owen and I talked about all three of us… But if he didn't share that part of the conversation with Kingston… This was making my head hurt. "If you could cut to the point, I'd love that, so I don't panic over what you do or don't mean."

Kingston smiled. It wasn't an arrogant kind of smirk, it was gentler. "Neither of us is willing to give you up, and both of us have too much invested in our own relationship to destroy that. So, when he gets back, all three of us are going to talk and figure out how we all fit together."

He didn't mention Owen's more-than-friendly feelings toward him. Had they talked about it? I wanted to know—possibly needed to—but it didn't feel like my place to bring it up.

"Sometimes you sound like him. All logical and stuff." I should have seen this coming. Owen and I had the beginning of this conversation. He was right, I needed to trust them more. Now seemed like a good time to actively work on that.

"I'll take that as the ultimate compliment." Kingston closed the distance between us, rested his hands on my hips, and pressed his body to mine.

I gasped into the kiss and draped my arms around his neck, locking my fingers together. Voices drifted in from the other room, but it was easy to block them out when I was wrapped up in Kingston.

"I was thinking"—his words hummed against my lips—"we could recreate that first night in here. I know it's only the two of us, but you've got frosting on hand…"

"I like the way you think. Everyone will be gone soon."

He dragged his nose up the side of my neck. "Why wait?"

A new flavor of discomfort crept into my veins, tugging on an old memory. "Because there are people out there. Someone could walk in here any moment."

"That's part of the fun. The thrill of the danger." Kingston fiddled with my buttons, undoing one.

My stomach recoiled at his touch. The sounds on the other side of the door turned to raucous laughter in my head. I pushed him away and stepped back. "I said *no.*"

Chapter Nineteen

My words came out more forcefully than I intended, but I was glad for the distance. Cool air rushed in, but it didn't soothe my nausea. I rebuttoned my shirt, hiding more skin than I had before.

"Okay. We'll wait." He studied me with concern.

I shook my head and stepped back farther, but the actions didn't stop the past from forcing its way to the front of my mind. The memory of— The laughter. The pointing. The humiliation. I choked on a sob. Why did this still have this impact on me?

"Lyn." Kingston kept his distance. "Talk to me?"

I couldn't tell him this. No one in my current life knew this story. Not Anne or Sadie…

He extended his hand. "Whatever's going through your head right now, it doesn't make me care about you any less. Whatever your reasons for telling me to stop. I'm sorry I didn't get it sooner. Tell me what you're thinking?"

asking for it

If I kept locking this away, I gave it power over me. I did want to trust Kingston, and this was a big thing. The worst he could do was laugh and agree with the people who... I frowned. "Can we go upstairs?" To get away from the people, and give me time to collect my thoughts.

"Of course."

I headed up first, uncomfortably conscious of whether or not I cared if he could see up my skirt. This was a man I was falling for, though. He had never been anything but adoring. Kind. Attentive. This wasn't the same as what happened back then.

I'd repeated *this isn't the same* enough times that when we reached my apartment, I could breathe again. I locked the door behind us. "You can sit." But I had too much nervous energy, so I was going to pace.

Kingston lingered nearby.

"So..." I laughed nervously as I exhaled. "This is probably stupid."

"Don't do that. It bothers you. It's not stupid."

Why did he have to be so sweet?

I clenched my first and forced my tongue to loosen. "I told you I used to dance." I could do this. It wasn't a big deal. "I was still the chubby girl in the group, but I was good." The words weren't going to stop until I finished. "I always danced without anything on under my tights, to avoid panty lines. A lot of the girls did. My boyfriend at the time—"

Bile rose in my throat and I swallowed it back. He wasn't just my boyfriend, he was also my first everything. Kiss. Making out until the car windows steamed up. Sex…

Kingston watched me, concern on his face.

Thankfully he didn't interrupt. I might not be able to finish if I lost more momentum. "He found out, and he thought it was hot. That's what he told me. I believed him. I believed everything he told me. We were doing a performance at school. In front of the entire auditorium. He rushed the stage, yanked down my bottoms, and exposed me to every single one of my classmates." I nearly gagged on the memory. "For the next two years, until my parents finally caved and moved me to a different school, every time I walked down the hall, someone would shout *Hey, Fattie Bush.*" Not the most creative taunt, but so painful to teenage me.

I forced myself to look at Kingston. The story was out there, it didn't control me, and I wouldn't cower away from the consequences.

His fists were clenched and his mouth drawn in a straight line. "I'm sorry. No one deserves that, but especially not you. I swear, if I ever meet that asshole, I'll pound his dick into the dirt with a baseball bat."

asking for it

The force and venom in his voice startled me, and I had to admit, seared away my blanket of doubt. "You'd go to jail for that."

"Worth it. There are a lot of things I'd do for you."

I ducked my head.

He placed a finger under my chin, forcing my gaze to his. "So, no public stuff. Nothing that risks us getting caught. I won't ask again," Kingston said. "But I will ask if I can stay tonight. You can keep the skirt on—and everything else—all night if it makes you feel better. I'm not assuming sex, I just want to be here, to hold you."

I laughed, to keep tears from escaping. "How are you so perfect?"

"I paid a witch two buttons and some pocket lint when I was five, and here we are." He took my hand and led me to the couch. "I'm happy to watch movies with you, or talk, or anything, as long as I get to hold you."

I curled up next to him tucked my feet to the side, and rested my head on his shoulder. When he draped an arm around me, I actually felt small. Safe. How did he do that?

We put on the newest Marvel movie, because we'd both only seen it twice.

Kingston trailed his fingers through my hair. "Since we're spilling secrets—not that mine is the same type as yours, but it changed my world—I talked to Owen today."

I frowned. "So you mentioned."

"About more than you."

I figured. He's your business partner. This was about something else, though. Kingston had let me get through my story, I'd do the same for him.

Kingston's hand stalled. "I was jealous when he said he was falling for you. Jealous both ways. You got something from him I've wanted for years, but never realized it until he told me. And then he said he loves me, and I said it back."

If this were an anime, this was the moment where I'd go pale like a ghost and get a giant sweat bead and know that I'd lost them both. After being terrified of exactly that for weeks, for different reasons, why wasn't the fear there now?

I sat up, needing to look Kingston in the eye for this conversation. "And?"

"It doesn't change how I feel about you." He cupped my cheek and searched my face. "I don't want to keep anything from you, but I don't want to push you away, either. I meant everything I said earlier. And you're not surprised or freaking out. Owen told you already."

I leaned into his touch. "It's kind of obvious, even with as little time as the three of us have spent together. But he also told me his half. Not yours."

asking for it

"And you're still here."

"It's my house."

Kingston rolled his eyes, but he was smiling. "Tell me what you're thinking."

"I'm thinking it's more of a revelation to the two of you than to me. I'm thinking I'd be a little hurt"—I didn't want to hold back. I wanted to be honest with him—"a lot hurt, if I lost you because of it. Either of you. Actually, it's kind of a relief."

He kissed me lightly. "Every time I think you can't get more amazing… So you think you could date both of us, while he and I are figuring things out with each other?"

Pretty sure that was what I'd been doing. It was nice to let myself put the label on it. "Looking forward to it. If we're having this conversation now, what are we supposed to talk to Owen about tomorrow?"

"Not sure I plan on talking much the next time I have both of you in a room together." He laid a series of playful nibbles along my bottom lip. "And we're missing the movie."

"Spoiler alert—the good guys win," I teased.

Kingston nudged me to lean back into him. "It's always about story more than the conclusion," he said.

I couldn't agree more.

I was aware of the good guys getting their asses kicked badly for the first time, and the next thing I knew, Kingston was shaking me gently.

"Hey." His voice was soft. "You missed the post credits scene."

I'd missed everything else, too. I forced some of the sleep from my eyes and sat up, mostly to stay conscious. "I keep falling asleep on you. You must think I'm the worst."

"Twice is hardly a habit." He stood and tugged me to my feet. "And I think you're the best."

"You're lucky you're cute, or I wouldn't let you get away with the endless flattery."

He tugged me toward the bedroom. "I'm lucky about a lot of things. *Cute* does make the list. I'm guessing it's more comfortable in here."

"It is. But I'm not sleeping in this." I fumbled with the buttons on my blouse. Great, I was too tired to undress myself.

"Here." Kingston kissed my knuckles, then gently pushed my hands aside. He removed my blouse and skirt, and draped them over the back of a nearby chair. "Bed. Now." He pulled back the comforter to expose the sheets.

I lay down. "Yes, sir."

I was half-aware of Kingston stripping off most of his clothes too. Shame I wasn't more awake to enjoy the show.

asking for it

He slipped into bed behind me, wrapped his arm around my waist, and pressed into my back. "Sweet dreams."

When I opened my eyes again, it was because sunlight was streaming through the window and warming my face.

Kingston had an arm draped over me and was pressed against my back. A specific part of him pressed harder than anything else, into one ass cheek.

A woman could get used to waking up like this. How selfish was I for wishing there were one other person here with us? Then it would be perfect.

"Good morning, gorgeous." Kingston's breath was hot against my shoulder.

I snuggled back into him. "It really is. Good, I mean. And morning too. I'm gonna stop talking now. At least until after coffee."

He laughed. "I have a better idea. Do you have any whipped cream? Chocolate sauce?"

"Downstairs. In the mood for sweet coffee?" I'd never seen him take more than cream and sugar before.

"Not quite. I want breakfast."

"Do you want anything with the whipped cream and chocolate? Waffles? Pancakes?"

Kingston kissed my shoulder. "You."

"Oh." Heat flooded my cheeks.

He untangled himself from the sheets. "Don't move."

"But—"

Kingston stepped into view. He was only wearing boxers, and *wow* that view. He held up a warning finger. "I'll be right back. Promise."

When I heard my apartment door open and close, I raised my eyebrows. He was actually going downstairs dressed like that. Insane. And loveable.

Was I actually thinking the *L* word about Kingston?

Yes. I couldn't put it into that little three word sentence, but… I couldn't deny anymore that thinking about him or Owen made a happy flutter in my chest.

Kingston returned quickly, proposed toppings in hand, and a bath towel draped over one arm. "Will you trust me?" he asked.

"I do." Saying that felt so good.

He tugged me to my feet, grabbed his shirt from the back of the chair it was draped over, and folded it over my eyes.

My heart hammered against my ribs at the loss of one sense. I strained my ears for any sound. The texture of the carpet against my feet was a sharp contrast to the sunshine on my cheek and the cool air on my arms.

asking for it

When Kingston trailed his fingers up my spine, I sucked in a sharp breath. "You can stop me any time." His voice was low and seductive.

I licked my lips, but couldn't find a response beyond nodding.

He stripped off my bra and panties, leaving me exposed and blind.

A spike of panic gripped my lungs.

His lips along my bare skin soothed me again. "Lay down."

At least I could climb into my own bed in the dark. But the texture was off. Rougher. The towel he'd fetched pressed into my bare skin. So many sensations I felt every day, but never paid attention to.

And we were just getting started.

The pause and absence of any sound or contact cranked my anticipation as much as the air on my exposed skin.

Lips brushed over mine, and I sighed. Cool liquid hit my nipples and I shifted to a gasp. The syrup flowed and pooled over my skin, and my pulse raced at the sensations.

Kingston dragged his tongue up my breastbone in a lazy path that teased around my breasts, up to my collar bone, and back down again. When he finally closed his mouth over one nipple, I whimpered.

He devoured one breast and then the other, licking me clean as if he were being graded and wanted a top score. A pause in his attention was punctuated by the hiss of the whipped cream can, and a new feathery light brush against my skin.

Then his mouth was back. Sucking and nibbling until I was clenching the sheets and whimpering.

"I love watching you." His words hummed against my skin. "Always, but especially when you're turned on. Your skin gets this stunning pink tinge. The way you bite your lower lip… *Christ* you do wicked things to me."

"Me? To you?" My laugh faded into another moan when he drizzled syrup down my stomach. A flash of self-consciousness vanished when his mouth followed the trail without hesitation.

He covered me in an alternating pattern of chocolate, whipped cream, and open mouthed kisses, over my hips, my thighs, and spreading my legs to lick along the inner skin.

I didn't know how much of the wetness pooling from me was syrup and how much was desire.

When he finally dragged his tongue along my slit, my hips bucked and I ground into his face. He plunged his tongue inside me, and my body gyrated in time to his attention. His thumb on my clit, circling and rubbing, over and over, time to his hungry licking, pushed me to orgasm.

Kingston eased his thumb away when I started to clench around him, then pressed back in again, drawing out my climax. Coaxing me until I was writhing in pleasure.

I collapsed back against the sheets with a breathless gasp. The darkness was comforting now. A way to sink into the mini tremors still tickling my senses.

The weight of Kingston's body covered mine. His kiss tasted like chocolate, whipped cream, and me, and was sloppy. Hungry. Uncontrolled.

"I need to be inside you," he managed between nibbles on my lips.

"Yes. Definitely yes."

I heard the tear of foil—a condom—and Kingston pushed my legs farther apart to kneel between.

It was so easy to lose myself in sensation this way. How good he felt sliding inside me. Gripping my thighs. Pushing my knees to my chest. And then pumping at a frantic pace.

He struck that sweet spot that yanked me toward orgasm again, and I clenched around him, clenched the sheets in my fists, clenched my toes when I came.

His grunts reached that delicious crescendo that meant he was close too. I'd missed that sound. It was more enticing that my favorite song.

The entire world seemed to pause when he slammed those last few, frantic thrusts against me, and then stopped.

He rested his cheek on my chest as we caught our breath. I had no idea how long we lay like that, but it didn't matter. This moment was as perfect as anything could be.

Kingston finally moved to strip off my makeshift blindfold, and kiss me. "I made a mess." His tone was playful and not the least bit apologetic.

There were traces of chocolate on us, on the towel… some had gotten on the sheets. I didn't care. I smiled and kissed him back. "I guess we need a shower."

"You're not going to get clean if we take one together."

"Then it'll have to be a long shower." I paused as the word flowed easily, waiting for that mental voice to remind me not to get too attached. To point out this would be over soon.

That nagging reminder wasn't there. I could imagine this lasting forever.

Chapter Twenty

I spent most of Sunday in bed with Kingston, and it was incredible. Not just the sex, though that was amazing, but his company and everything about the day.

The only thing that would have made it better was Owen being there. How was this my life, that I not only had that option, but there was so little angst between the three of us to agree it was a good next step?

I hated to send Kingston home Monday morning, but we had work. The fact that Owen texted and said he'd be back tonight instead of tomorrow made parting more bearable.

I didn't try to ignore the anticipation of the evening as I baked for the day. *We need to talk* had never been more appealing.

It was my day to balance the books from the week before, and we'd done even better at Saturday's event than I realized. I'd be making an extra loan payment to the bank this month.

A little before noon, I grabbed myself some lunch—I'd probably had more pastries in the last month than I should have, but today seemed like a good day for another one, to help with paperwork.

Just after two, there was a knock on my office door, and Violet poked her head in. "Do you know Ramsey Miller?"

"Mhm. Why?"

"He's here to see you, and he asked for Lyn."

I pushed back from my desk. "I met him a few weeks ago. Nice guy."

"He's really not." Violet scowled.

Weird. "Fill me in, after I talk to him."

Violet followed me out to the café, where Ramsey sat at one of the tables.

He grinned and stood when he saw me. "Hey. How have you been?"

"Good." *Fantastic. Incredible. Amazing.* "You?" I wasn't close enough with him to give him any more than a polite answer, no matter how much I'd enjoyed his and Ravyn's company.

"Good. Good. Normally we have a constable deliver these, but I wanted to say *hi* and try the coffee and chocolate croissant—amazing but the way." He handed me an envelope.

Nervousness whispered at the edge of my mind. "Constable? Am I in trouble?" I forced a light laugh.

asking for it

His chuckle sounded genuine. "Nothing like
that. The zoning hearing on your building has been
bumped up to Wednesday. Not that you're going to
fight it, but notifying you is a formality."

"Why wouldn't I fight it?" My blood was icing
over in my veins.

Ramsey's smile slipped. "Because you're
selling? Making things *official* with Kingston?"

My gut flipped in on itself. I should have
skipped lunch. "Did he tell you that?"

"Not in so many words, but he never stops
talking about you. He did tell you I was pushing—
Fuck. He didn't tell you."

I couldn't speak. Where was my wit? My
venom? Why wasn't I biting back?

"Didn't tell her what?" The fury in Violet's
question mirrored what I felt.

Thank the heavens for Violet.

Ramsey set the letter on the table. "I shouldn't
say anything else."

"Finish the thought." I found my voice, and
forced it out through a raw throat. I was fucking scary
when I was pissed off.

"Kingston filed the petition to change the
zoning. When the request came in today to push the
date up, I figured it was because the two of you are...
He would have told you... *Fuck.*"

My world spun. I was going to be ill. Would projectile vomiting on Ramsey be more humiliating than what I'd been through in the last month? Were Kingston and Owen laughing about this right now?

"You're such a raging fucking tool." Violet's voice grew in volume as she stepped toward Ramsey. "I always knew, but this... You fucking asshole. People like you are the reason the system—"

I settled a hand on her arm, and used the pause to find that same ice to force through all of me. I wouldn't break. Not in front of him, and sure as hell not in front of Kingston and Owen when I confronted them. I picked up the notice from the table. "Consider me served. Thank you for letting me know. I'll be there."

"I really am sorry." Ramsey sounded sincere.

Like I was ever buying that kind of bullshit again.

"If you were sorry, you'd take it back," Violet said.

He fixed a glare on her. "It doesn't work that way."

"Why not? Can *I* call in a favor? You sadistic fuckhole." Violet was yelling now.

I tightened my grip on her arm. "It's okay. Let him leave. I do have a favor though, Ramsey."

"If I can," he said.

"Don't tell Kingston we talked?" I kept my tone sweetly submissive. "I don't want to cause any ripples between us."

Ramsey's smile wasn't so confident now. "Of course. I'd rather not step between that anyway."

"Thank you." I was calm now. At least on the surface. What raged underneath... I was saving that.

Chapter Twenty-One

I vanished into my office again. As soon as the door swung shut behind me, tears of frustration and disbelief tried to force their way out.

I wouldn't cry. I wouldn't fall apart. They weren't worth that.

It took far too long to collect myself, and then I sent Kingston and Owen a message. *Excited about tonight.* Thankfully bitterness didn't carry across texts. *Can we meet at one of your hotel rooms?*

Kingston's answer came in seconds later. *Mine. Miss you. See you then.*

I clenched my fist so tightly my nails dug into my palm, and summoned more calm.

Miss you too. See you then. I could pretend to care as well as they could. At least for the next couple of hours.

I wrapped up work a little early, to get ready. It was tempting to wear something I could hide in. The baggier the better.

asking for it

They didn't get to see me shrink away, though. I would never again hide from someone trying to humiliate me.

I dressed in one of my more flattering shirts. Something that gave me nice cleavage. Took the attention away from the trouble spots.

Fat. You mean the fat. Call it what it is.

I wouldn't fall into that pit. Not tonight. I couldn't afford to.

Doesn't matter what you wear. They don't care. This was all a joke for them. You're a joke.

No. I forced the taunting aside.

On the drive to their hotel, I kept the music loud enough to drown out my thoughts. It took more will than I had to climb from the car, take the elevator to their floor, and walk down the hall to Kingston's room.

I forced myself to breathe when I knocked.

Kingston opened the door with the biggest, sweetest smile ever, and the careful wall I'd been building all day almost shattered. He stepped aside to let me in, and the instant the door closed behind us, he spun me to face him.

I planted a palm on his chest, and shoved him back, stepping farther into the room to find that Owen was there too. Perfect. I could sever both ties at once.

"What's wrong?" Kingston looked hurt.

Good. Fuck him. Or not. Never again, in fact. "Are you familiar with zoning laws in this city?" I was still cool. Calm. Ice.

"Shit." Owen's exclamation almost undid me. "You were supposed to tell her."

I focused a deadly sweet smile on him. "Tell me what?"

"Depends on what you know." If Kingston was trying to sound flippant, he failed.

I was glaring by the time I turned his way. "It shouldn't. You should have told me from the start. But that would ruin the fun, wouldn't it? Sorry, let me back up. Did you know the zoning on my building is being challenged?" I felt no satisfaction when Kingston winced. "I talked to Ramsey Miller today. He stopped by to tell me in person, because the two of you are such great friends, that the hearing to decide if they'd kick me out of my house or not had been moved up to two days from now. At your request, just like the original filing was."

"What? No." Kingston managed to sound genuinely surprised.

I wasn't. He'd been lying to my face about everything for more than a month. "You didn't file for a zoning change?"

He grimaced. "I did, but I figured I still had a few days to fess up."

"And by then it wouldn't matter? Because you'd have suckered me into thinking you care?" My retort held a sharp edge. "Maybe you shouldn't have pulled strings to move up the hearing date, in that case."

"I didn't do that. I promise."

I let out a barking laugh. "Oh, then it's okay. We're okay. None of this matters."

"Kitty Cat—"

"Don't." I whirled on Owen again. "Don't call me that. And don't think you can use logic to convince me this isn't a big deal. You fucked me. Both of you. To get to my shop. This was the plan from the start, wasn't it? Pick me up at the bookstore—"

"We didn't know who you were," Owen said.

I looked at Kingston. This was going to give me whiplash. "Didn't you?"

"Hand to God." He had the nerve to raise his fucking hand.

I shook my head in disbelief. "Like that means anything coming from you. Like I trust a single word you say. It's just a complete and total coincidence that I got the zoning change notice the same night you *found* me in the coffee shop? And the next morning you *just happened* to walk into my café, when the pick-up didn't work? You figured, fuck the fat chick, and she'll do anything we ask?"

Anger bled onto Kingston's face.

"I promise you—"

"Or was this a fetish?" I cut Owen off again. I could probably scream at Kingston all night, but if Owen started talking, if he was reasonable, I didn't know if I'd have a counter. I wouldn't be shut down. "A game, maybe? Let's fuck the fat—"

"Stop." Kingston's voice was hard. "Don't call yourself that."

Seriously? "Fuck you. You don't get to say what I do. I can call myself fa—"

"No. Because you're not." Kingston was definitely mad. Good. "You're intelligent. You're fun. You're gorgeous."

"I'm gullible. I'm easy to lie to. I'm desperate for a connection. Why don't you say what you're really thinking?" Why did this hurt so much?

Owen reached for my arm and I jerked away with a glare.

He held up his hands and kept his distance. "You'll probably take this the wrong way, but your shop isn't worth what you're accusing us of."

I barked in disbelief. "Is there a right way to take that?"

"No one's shop is worth that. Why would either of us, let alone both of us, spend a month leading you on, for a little café?"

asking for it

"*Wow*, you're shit at apologies. Or do you just want to twist the knife a little more? The deception isn't complete until I'm bleeding?"

Owen's expression was blank, but if I looked close enough, I swore I could see a barely controlled emotion under the surface. "You know me better than that."

"Do I? Is the two of you *falling for each other* part of the game? A way to draw me in? A way out? *Sorry, Baby, now that we have what we want, we love each other. Bye.*" Even as I spit out the sarcasm, I knew that last bit wasn't true. But if it was real, other things they were saying may be too, and I couldn't accept that.

Owen pulled off a spectacular imitation of hurt mixed with anger. "The only reason to do what we did, either of us, with you, is because we love your company. Not as in your business, but spending time with *you*. I was genuine—we both were. I love everything about you."

"You don't get to say that to me. Not now. Not ever." I was shredded from the inside-out. "You lied to me the moment you approached me. You didn't even give me your real names. I should have known everything after that would be just as much bullshit. I should have—" I choked off a sob. *Don't break. Not here. Not in front of them.*

I forced myself to breathe. To look calm, despite crumbling. "This charade, joke, whatever it is, it's over. Don't set foot in my store again. Don't call me again. We're done."

I spun on my toe and stalked toward the door. It was tempting to bump Kingston with my shoulder on my way past, but I didn't want to feel him ever again, even for that.

"Lyn." Pleading hung heavy in his voice, hitting my back. "Please. I love you."

Thank God he couldn't see me. I didn't pause as I walked out of the room, down the back stairs, and to my car. I made it out of the parking lot, and all the way to the bookstore before I had to pull over. I couldn't see the road through the tears streaming down my face.

How could I have been such an idiot?

Chapter Twenty-Two

I didn't sleep that night. I tried, but the dreams were torture. A blend of school and now, people—Kingston and Owen—laughing at me. Stripping me bare. Exposing me to the world.

I gave up around three in the morning, downed half a pot of coffee, and made my way to the café kitchen. Now seemed like as good a time as any to bake new recipes for customers to try.

I burned the first couple, staring off into space. That made the taunting in my head worse.

With some more coffee, I was ready to go.

I lost track of time as I lost myself in cooking. Whenever my stomach growled or my eyelids drooped, more coffee.

"Lyn?" Anne's concerned tone drew me out of my haze.

I instinctively painted on a smile when I looked up at her. "Hey. What are you doing here? It's the middle of the day." It was, wasn't it? Sun was streaming through the windows, and not low in the sky.

"Violet called me. She said something happened yesterday, and she's worried about you."

"I'm fine." My voice cracked. "Just tired." A shudder ran through me, and tears tried to force their way out.

Anne pulled up a stool next to mine, wrapped an arm around my shoulder, and pulled me into her in a half hug. "Why didn't you call?"

"I don't know. I didn't want to be a bother. You have your life. Your guys. So does Sadie." Tears were flowing freely again. I didn't want to be crying. Why couldn't I stop?

"We're always here for you."

They shouldn't be. I made this mistake. It wasn't their responsibility to drop everything and console me for being blind. "They used me. They told me up front that they were going to win me over as a business partner, and I pushed my doubts aside. I thought it meant more. I'm such an idiot."

"You're not." Anne shifted and pulled me closer, hugging me tight. "This isn't your fault."

"But it is. I knew who they were, what they wanted, and I pretended what we had was something else."

"If it was me that this happened to, would you tell me it was my fault?"

"I don't know."

asking for it

"But you do," Anne said gently. "You know and I know this isn't on you. They lied. It's not up to you to read between the lines every time. You have to trust people sometimes, and it's their fault for breaking that trust. You're more than that. You deserve better."

I wasn't sure I agreed with that last bit. I leaned into her, sobbing and unable to grasp more words.

She held me until I was done, then got me a damp paper towel to wash my face, and something to drink.

"What are we doing tonight?" Anne asked.

"I'm going to curl up in a ball and vanish." The crying was inevitable, but it didn't help me feel better.

Anne stood and tugged me to my feet. "Then I'll stay with you while you do that."

"If you're here, then technically I haven't vanished." I followed her upstairs, lacking the strength to protest.

"Then I guess I can't let you vanish."

The words were enough to tug more tears loose. Would I ever stop crying?

Anne loaded one action movie after another, always picking those with no romance. She ordered pizza, but I couldn't stomach food. I nibbled a couple of bites to keep her happy, and couldn't manage more.

She fell asleep, head in my lap, around midnight. I gently moved her aside to make some coffee. If my dreams were going to be the same as last night, I wasn't having it.

By the time the sun rose, I'd numbed the pain enough to do something resembling functioning. Anne offered to go to the zoning hearing with me, but I shooed her off to work. She was busy, and I refused to let her miss two days in a row because I'd given my hea— Made a mistake with who I trusted.

Neither Kingston nor Owen was at the hearing. Because no one showed to argue for changing the zoning, and because I had my paperwork in order to show why it should stay as-is, the request was dismissed.

Arrogant idiots. All that trouble for nothing, on their part.

Unless Kingston never intended to pursue it after we got close.

I couldn't believe that. Refused. It was the only way to cling to any bit of sanity.

As I was leaving, Ramsey caught up to me.

"Hey, I heard you guys split," he said.

I smiled too brightly. Toning it down meant falling apart. "Split implies what we had was real." Was it better or worse that I said with so much enthusiasm and cheer?

asking for it

Ramsey shook his head. "I'm glad things went your way. I love the café, and you shouldn't have to change how you do business."

"Thank you." I was too much sunshine, but I couldn't lower the glare. "Can I do anything else for you?"

"I wanted you to know, it wasn't Kingston who pushed the hearing up. I assumed, and I shouldn't have. The clerk said it was one-hundred percent a scheduling issue."

"That's fine. I need to run. Have a fantastic day."

Ramsey's smile was weak. "You too."

I was numb. I wasn't thinking about Kingston and Owen. The only way to get through this was to stay icy until the pain receded. On the way home, I stopped at the grocery store. The ice cream called my name, and I'd forgotten to sneak in an order with my supplier. But I still hated that I ate so much last time. I grabbed a box of sugar free ice pops instead. Those would hit my sweet tooth perfectly, and keep me from getting dehydrated from the coffee I also stocked up on.

Every time I dozed off, as the night wore on, the nightmares rushed back. That coffee was a lifesaver.

I was more alert on Thursday. The world around me was in focus, and all I had to do was keeping looking forward. And drink more coffee.

Friday was more of the same, but I was up for getting back to the books. I wouldn't let my café crumble from neglect, after keeping it out the hands of… assholes.

I logged into my banking portal to make my extra loan payment—it still felt good to be able to do so, as long as I ignored the memories of how that night ended.

My loan balance was at zero.

Odd.

Software glitch? All of my other accounts looked right. I could check back in a few hours, but a quick call to the bank would clear things up.

The woman who answered was cheerful. She probably meant to sound pleasant, but the sincerity grated on me. Did she mean it? What was she hiding from the world, under that brightness?

I couldn't go through life questioning everyone who sounded like they meant something. "Hi. I'm calling because my loan balance isn't showing correctly on the website." I gave her my name and account number.

"I can check that for you, hang on." The clacking of keys filled otherwise dead air. "Miss?"

"I'm still here."

"Your account is fine. I show the loan paid off. I'm not sure why it's not reflecting that for you, but give it a few hours—"

asking for it

"I'm sorry." I couldn't have heard her correctly. "I didn't pay off my loan. I wish I had, but no."

"Oh." More clacking keys. "Can I put you on hold for a moment?"

"Of course."

I didn't want to deal with this today, but it was better than what I'd been mired in. At least this was a problem I could confront head-on. Something I could get a solution for.

After a few minutes, the hold music vanished. "Jaelyn?" Miss Cheerful was back.

"Yes?"

"There's no mistake. We received your check, drawn from Kingu Kafes, for the full balance this morning."

Fuckers. "That's right. I forgot they were sending that today. I'm so sorry to take up your time."

"It's fine. Is there anything else I can do for you?"

Castrate the last two men I slept with. "No, thank you so much." I disconnected.

I was so livid, I was seeing red. Apparently that was a thing. My anger had me swaying on my feet. How *dare* they? I could call and scream, but I wanted to look them in the eye and ask them *what the actual hell?* They couldn't buy their way into my life any more than they could fuck their way into my café.

I made it to their hotel and was hammering the side of my fist on Kingston's door before I registered confronting them in person wasn't the best idea for me right now. They probably weren't here anyway.

When Kingston answered the door, surprise on his face, my stomach crumpled. If it hadn't been empty, I might have vomited on his shoes.

"Lyn." He sounded relieved.

I was angry. And tired. But mostly angry. I shoved past him, stalling for a heartbeat when I saw Owen was there too, sitting at the desk. "What are you doing?" I demanded.

"Working?" Leave it to Owen to be understatedly direct.

I wasn't in the mood. The room was wobbly—did anger do that? "With my loan. You can't just go around paying off people's loans. If you thought I was pissed about being fucked to get into my good graces, large sums of money I didn't ask for, in addition to the sex, aren't going to help."

"This isn't about sex," Owen said. "It's not about your shop, or our business. It's a gift. There's no lienholder. We don't have any claim to anything you own."

Kingston moved into view and stood next to Owen. "We want you to be successful and happy."

asking for it

"Oh, okay. Sure." Sarcasm bled into my retort. "And I'm supposed to believe that? How do I know this isn't a way to get back into my life?"

"It's not. I'm telling the truth. Why do you have such a hard time believing we like you for you?" Owen's typical calm demeanor was buried under a frown.

My brain stalled on his question, and I forced the gears to start turning again. "But you didn't tell me the truth." That was the problem. The root of all of this.

Kingston pulled out a spare chair. "Sit, please? We'll talk." When I shook my head, he stayed standing "I'm sorry I put off telling you about the zoning. But that was the only—"

"The only lie? That and the names? One of the very first things you said to me when we met face to face? *Barney*? Your track record speaks for itself." Maybe I should take the chair. Four nights of no sleep was catching up to me.

"I'm sorry," Kingston said. "*We're* sorry. It was a dick move anyway, but I hate that it was done to you."

I wasn't hearing that no-fault bullshit. "That *you* did it to me. This wasn't a generic fluke; *you* made it happen."

Owen sighed. "You're right, we did."

"Ravyn and Ramsey told me you don't call in favors." I focused on him. Or tried to. He was kind of fuzzy around the edges. "Guess I was special?"

"You are special. There were no favors." Kingston looked blurry too. "I filed a request for a zoning change. Anyone could have done it."

"I tried to have it pulled after we met you. I would have used a favor for that, but Ramsey couldn't make it happen. We had to let it go to hearing," Owen said.

I should shut this down and go home. Why was I here? "Goodie for you. You did something cruel, and then couldn't backstep it. Boo hoo."

Owen's frown deepened. "I'm sorry. I miss you."

Why did he have to sound so sincere? It made me want to punch something.

"Give us another chance," Kingston said.

"How many chances do I give you?" Darkness licked the corners of my vision. I was definitely wobbling. And so tired. "I think I'll take that seat now." My world went black.

Chapter Twenty-Three

Why was I in a hospital bed? An IV running into my arm?

Everything in my brain was fuzzy. I'd been furious at Kingston and Owen. Yelling. Wobbling.

Someone kept asking me questions. My head throbbed as I tried to make sense of the memories. Was I taking any medications? Any allergies? When was the last time I ate? That was easy. Days ago. Unless coffee counted.

"…leave when we… answers." Owen? He was shouting, but I couldn't make out all the words. Owen shouted?

"…deserve answers… what you did… Fuck you both." That was Anne. She sounded pissed.

"I'll help you find the door." Luke's voice was more distinct. Or carried better. Or I was becoming more aware.

The pain shooting through the back of my neck said the latter was definitely the case.

"*No.*" Kingston's reply was easy to make out. I could picture him stubborn and squaring off against

Luke's six-foot-two of imposing former Marine. I wasn't surprised Kingston didn't back down.

"Sirs, please."

I didn't know that voice.

"Tell Lyn," Owen called.

"No." And that was Sadie.

Was the entire world here? For me? What had I done? I didn't want this attention. I wanted to curl up in a ball and vanish.

A beeping noise sounded next to my ear. Great, now what?

A nurse appeared by my side almost immediately, looked at something near me, then at me. "It's a blood oxygen monitor. I need you to take a deep breath."

"Why am I here?"

"Take a deep breath." She was sterner this time.

I complied, mostly to get this part over with.

"Now exhale slowly, and repeat," she said.

I didn't have the patience for this, but after several excruciatingly slow inhales and exhales, the beeping stopped.

"I'm Joy. What do you remember?"

"I'm not sure. It's all jumbled."

Joy nodded. "A sign of exhaustion. Keep breathing. Your friend told 911 that you passed out. In the ambulance, you told the EMT you hadn't eaten or slept since Monday."

asking for it

"I was delirious. I didn't mean that." Crap, I didn't want to be stuck here. I started to sit. The alarm went off again.

Joy nudged me back gently. "Your blood tests show low potassium and some other nutrients, and you're dehydrated, so I suspect at least some of it's true. Keep breathing, or I'll have to put you on oxygen."

I made a show of taking and letting out several deep breaths.

"Good." She smiled. "Your friends don't know what happened—privacy laws—and I can't let them all in here at once. Who do you want to see?"

"Can I see two of them? Sadie and Anne. Purple hair, and blonde?"

"All right."

A moment later, Anne and Sadie appeared in my doorway, and then I was wrapped in hugs.

"We were so worried." Anne squeezed me tighter. "You're okay, aren't you?"

I was going to cry again, at their concern, and I didn't want to. Aside from that I was okay. "I'm fine. How did you know…?"

Sadie made herself comfortable next to me on the bed. "Kingston slid into my DM's. Said he didn't know how to get hold of any of your friends. I waited until I was here, and knew you were safe, and could look him in the eye before I told him what I thought of him."

"The yelling in the hallway?" I put some pieces together.

Anne nodded. "Luke is out there standing guard. What happened?"

"Long story. I had to see them about something, I was more tired than I thought…" Shit. The shop. "I need to get home. There's baking to do. Other work."

"The doctor's not ready to discharge you," Joy said from the doorway.

Sadie leaned into me. She did a decent job of making pinning me down look like a hug. "I already called Violet," she said. "The café will have to go without pastries for a day. It'll be okay."

"No. I can't. I—"

"Stop." Anne's voice was sharp. "You can. You will. If you're good, maybe we and the doctor will let you do a little work on Monday."

Sadie pulled out her phone. "Now, call your mom. Tell her you're all right."

"You told my mother?" Another person worrying about me who didn't have to.

Sadie pressed the phone to my ear. "You're in the hospital. Of course I told her."

"Hello?" Mama sounded concerned.

asking for it

And now my heart was cracking at her voice. Did exhaustion make someone cry about everything? "Hey, Mama."

"Jaelyn. How are you? What's wrong? Your friend told me you were in trouble. I'm trying to book a flight out there now.""

As much as I wanted to see my parents, I didn't want them paying last-minute flight prices. "I'm okay. I promise. I'll get the doctor to tell you so, too, if you need to hear it."

We chatted for a few more minutes, and I promised her I'd eat and sleep more, and convinced her not to change their vacation schedule for this. I'd see them in a few months. She asked for Sadie, and I handed over the phone.

Sadie's replies were mostly *yes* or a variation of it. By the time she gave me the phone again, my curiosity was at capacity.

"What did you tell her?" I asked my mom.

"To take care of you, and not to leave your side, and that if this happens again, we're hopping the next plane there."

"Yes, Mama."

"Love you. Dad loves you. Be safe."

I smiled. "Love you both too." I disconnected.

The doctor came to talk to me, and I told him it was fine if he did so in front of Anne and Sadie. I regretted the decision when he brought up the not eating or sleeping thing. He refused to discharge me if I was going home alone.

"That's not a problem," Sadie said, before I could argue. "I'm moving in with her for at least a couple of weeks. She won't be alone."

I gave her my best *excuse me?* look.

She shrugged. "I promised your mom. I have to. Besides, you take care of us all the time. You listen to us. You feed us. Over advice and hugs and support. We're here to do the same for you. Always. You just have to ask, or in this case, you don't even have to do that."

More tears stung my eyelids at the warmth that raced through me. I really did have the best friends in the world.

When Sadie and I got back to my place, she set her bags in her old room. "You didn't change much."

"I haven't gotten around to it." It wasn't that I cared if she knew I missed her, but I was already taking up her time. I didn't need to be clingy or sound like I was pulling a guilt trip on top of that.

"You missed me." Sadie grinned. She grabbed my hand and led me into the kitchen. "Sit."

I pulled up a chair at the kitchen table. "You have your own life." Weak comeback.

"That you're a part of. Where's all the food?"

asking for it

"I have plenty of food."

Sadie pulled a half-empty box of rice cakes from the cupboard, and a mostly full box of ice pops from the freezer. "Do you make sandwiches with these?"

I clenched my jaw. The last thing I wanted right now was a lecture on my eating habits.

Sadie grabbed her phone. "Pizza or Chinese?"

"Pizza." Not Chinese. Not again for a long time. The pit in my chest ached at the thought. How many other memories had been tainted?

Sadie made a few more swipes, than dropped into a chair across from me. "Ordered. You're in idiot, by the way." She met my gaze unflinchingly.

What was I supposed to say to that? Only I got to call me names. "Excuse me?"

"You heard me."

Because I'd fallen for the bull Owen and Kingston fed me? "What happened isn't my—"

"It's not your fault, I know. I agree. The stuff with those assholes? Not your fault in the slightest. "The not eating? The shutting us out so you're *not a bother*? That's on you."

Unbelievable. "This is your idea of supporting me?"

"You're one of us, Lyn. You're not a burden or a third wheel. We want you in our lives because we like you for you."

I didn't care for her plucking thoughts out of my head that were meant for me alone. "That's not what this is about."

Sadie raised her brows. "Isn't it?"

"No." Maybe a little?

"I'm not trying to be mean," Sadie said. "But I'm not taking back what I said."

"You called me an idiot." Like I hadn't done the same to myself countless times.

She didn't flinch. "*Idiot* was harsh, but I needed you to listen. You can be heartbroken. Take all the time you need to heal. You deserve so much more than being led on. You're worth more than that." She sighed. "My point is I wish I could show you what we see in you."

I didn't know what to say, and I was tired of feeling. "I'm going to lay down until the pizza gets here." I pushed back from the table.

"Wait." Sadie grabbed my wrist before I could walk away. She stood and threw her arms around me and squeezed tight. "You're amazing and wonderful and smart and successful and beautiful and so many other words that would take me all night and into next week to list. No one, not even you, should be allowed to tell you otherwise."

I didn't know what to do besides hug back, and fail to swallow past the lump in my throat.

———

The first thing I did Monday morning was drop a check in the mail, for a normal loan payment amount, addressed to Kingu Kafe's corporate offices. I couldn't pay them back all at once, but there was no way in hell I was taking anything from Kingston and Owen, especially money.

Sadie became my shadow, going so far as to get up when I did, and make me breakfast. I'm pretty sure she would have force fed me if I hadn't eaten voluntarily. With her company, it was easy to distract myself from my thoughts.

On Friday, a letter arrived from Kingu Kafe. My torn up check was inside, along with a note written in simple block letters. *The money was a gift. Non-returnable. We miss you. Owen.*

I used a baking blow torch to light the entire thing on fire in a steel bowl in the café's kitchen, while Sadie watched.

"Are you going to send them another one?" she asked.

It was tempting. "What do you think the odds are they'll send it back the same way?"

"Is either of them as stubborn as you?" Her question was kind.

I twisted my mouth in disbelief. "Do you remember who they were before..." The playful retort turned to ashes in my mouth. *Before they decided to stop asking to buy me out, and moved to using me instead?* "I'm done dealing with them."

The next week, I fell back into more of my routine. Except, every time I thought of Kingston and Owen, my heart cracked.

Though technically, I was almost always thinking about them. I missed them so desperately. My mind and heart never stopped arguing over *I love them* versus *they lied to me. About something huge.* Even worse, I never knew which part of me would take which side.

Violet, Sadie, and I were sitting around the café after it closed, taking our time cleaning up for the evening. Sadie would probably head back home in a few days. Which was fair, her husbands missed her, like I would when she was gone.

She and Anne already had a schedule worked out, to make sure I *behaved.* I'd assured them that was unnecessary, but I did appreciate the concern.

Violet finished putting up the last of the chairs, save for those we were sitting in, and joined Sadie and I at a table near the counter. We were discussing the café's next Cosplay Saturday, and whether we should have a set theme, with Sadie providing costumes. Something I was happy to spend a little extra business money on, for both her and my employees.

asking for it

"You're dressing up again." Sadie wasn't asking.

And there was another shitty memory. I exposed so much more of myself than my body at the end of that day. "No."

"You were glowing last time," Violet said.

"Because—" an attractive man told me I was pretty. "No."

Sadie scowled. "You rocked that skirt. You put so many of my peers to shame."

"But not you." I let a hint of bitterness into my retort.

"Including me. You were a goddess. And it wasn't because some guy was here."

"No, but it was because some guy lied about how he felt about me, and I believed the bullshit."

"Did he?" Sadie countered. "I know he kept something from you. But that doesn't mean he lied about all of it. And if he did, fuck that guy. His faults don't change how incredible you are."

"A lot of my kids struggle with who they are versus who the world tells them they should be." Violet's statement came out of nowhere. Her *kids* weren't actually her children—she volunteered at an LGBTQ+ shelter for teenagers when she wasn't here.

I had no idea how she found the time for all of it, but I understood being driven to keep busy. "I can see how that would be a common theme." I was missing a connection between her statement and our conversation. "Do they… turn to cosplay?" How idiotic did I sound right now?

Violet smiled. "Sometimes. Everyone copes differently. A lot of them, when they lose the support of people who were supposed to love them, because the kids don't meet that pre-defined mold, don't know where to find the line anymore between a forgivable slight and an unforgivable action."

"Ah." She was talking about me. "I'm fat. I'm insecure. I screwed out of my league. Not even in the same ballpark as someone's parents turning their backs on them for who they love."

"I don't pass judgment on the severity of the hurt, only that people hurt. You and they both blame things on being who you are, and it's not your fault."

I saw where she was coming from, but I disagreed. "It's not—"

"The same?" Violet finished for me. "How many times in your life have you diminished your pain, because you don't think you've earned the right to feel?"

I didn't have a response, beyond *you don't understand*, and something told me that wouldn't cut it. This wasn't as bad as trying to take the opposing point against Owen, but it was close.

asking for it

I missed Owen. An ache throbbed behind my ribs. Shouldn't I be numb to that now?

Violet studied me. "Nothing? You can say whatever you're thinking. I'm listening. I'll hear you."

And now Kingston was in my head, too. Telling me he wanted to get to know me for me, not to take my business. I gasped on a sob. Why couldn't I stop thinking about them?

I shook my head, unsure how to process any of this. It hurt, and someone was the cause of it. I let it happen. "Why can't I make this empty pit in my chest go away?"

"Sometimes life hurts." Sadie covered my hand with hers.

I knew that, but, "I was hoping for a more actionable answer. I thought they were sincere. They sounded… It felt…" *Real.* Even now, I swore the connection between all of us was real.

"Some people are good liars, and some people just make mistakes," Sadie said. "It's not always easy to tell which is which."

Violet nodded. "I agree. But here's the thing, I've rarely seen you happier than you were last Cosplay Saturday. During the day, in that gorgeous outfit. Not like someone hiding or hoping if they played by the right rules, things would be okay. You opened up. If you got to that point because of

Kingston, that's one thing he did right. But you're that person even without him."

"And that was part of the problem." A *big* part of the problem. I opened myself up to them. "I don't want to believe they did this maliciously." Now that I was talking, my jumbled thoughts from the last few weeks spilled out without much order. "But of course I don't want to. What I want doesn't change what is."

"People can make mistakes and learn and grow," Violet said.

"And sometimes people make a bad judgment call, because they make mistakes, not because they're bad people," Sadie added. "And sometimes people who have been hurt have a hard time accepting that others love them for them, without ulterior motive."

I glared at Sadie. "I'm starting to think you're not on my side."

"Then you're not paying attention." Sadie didn't flinch. "Maybe they used you, maybe they didn't. You assumed the *probably* awfully fast, and I'm trying to tell you it's not the only option."

I scrubbed my face, and blew out a noisy breath through my fingers. "I don't know what to do." I *wanted* to undo the bad, and only have the good. "Sometimes I have this almost irresistible impulse to talk to them again. Not to forgive them, but just to hear their voices." Sometimes. Every waking moment. Whatever. "That's a bad idea, isn't it?"

"It might be. There are times when it's best to avoid the people at all costs who hurt us. Other times, reaching out is the only way to heal." Violet was making good use of her therapy training. Of course she was putting it back on me to make a decision.

I was grateful for that, and at the same time resented it. I wanted an easy answer. "Those people we should avoid… do they change their business plan for the person they hurt, to avoid doing it again? Do they pay off hundreds of thousands of dollars in debt, without demanding something in return?"

Violet shook her head. "There's always a price attached to anything from the *avoid them at all costs* people, no matter how generous the act looks."

"I can see why you let her run things." Sadie leaned her head on my shoulder. "She's smart. I don't have quite such eloquent words, but Violet is right that you were happy with them. You were *you*. I'm sure they won't be your only chance at that, and I'm not saying they weren't wrong. I don't know if I could forgive them. I want you to do what will hurt you the least now, and later."

"Me too. Go figure." I let out a short laugh.

I still didn't have answers, though. And I still hurt, both thinking about how Kingston and Owen lied to me, and thinking about how much I missed them. But at least I had my girls, and myself, even if Sadie was pushing this whole agenda of self-worth pretty hard.

Chapter Twenty-Four

I sat in the front passenger seat of Anne's Ford Escape, staring at the shop across the street from us. The sign was an alteration on the original Kingu Kafe logo, to remove the heavier anime elements. The banner underneath said *Grand Opening*.

Sadie leaned forward from the back seat. "It looks basic."

"It's just a coffee shop. It doesn't have to be more than basic," Anne said.

We should turn around and go home. The thought had taunted me for the last hour, as we drove up here.

I'd heard rumors that Kingu was opening a new shop, and I tried to ignore the chatter. It hurt that they'd gone through with it anyway, but it was their original plan—open a new location here, regardless of if it was mine or a different one.

The invitation that arrived in my mail was probably meant just for me, given that address was hand lettered, and so was the brief note inside, in the same handwriting as the note from Owen returning my check weeks ago.

I wanted to be surprised at the personal invite and at the details of this place. Nearly fifty miles from my shop, in a different county, and it wasn't an anime gaming café. Like Anne said, it was just a coffee shop.

The part of my brain that had been listening to Sadie said this was more proof they cared about *me*, not my shop.

Their parking lot was packed, which made sense. They had a name, even if they were only serving coffee. But them putting up a place like this was no more competition for me than a Starbucks would be in the same location.

I'd gone back and forth since about whether or not I wanted to come.

"We can go home," Anne said. "You saw."

But now that I was here, I wanted to see *them*. Of course, that would lead to wanting to talk to them, which could lead to… what?

If they'd been using me for my shop, and they brushed me off now, at least I'd know. If they liked me for me…

"I want to see what it looks like inside." I had no idea anymore what was a mistake. "But I'll stay in back. I just want to see what they've done, and then we'll go."

The interior was beautiful—anime meets abstract. Owen and Kingston's influences were evident in the decor, borrowing from what I'd seen of their other shops, but it was also its own unique design. If someone told me the shop owners were usually my competition, I wouldn't believe them.

When my gaze fell on Kingston working the register, any thoughts about my environment vanished in a surge of longing tinged with pain. He was smiling, chatting, and sexier than I remembered.

Which was saying a lot.

I dragged my attention away long enough to search out Owen, but I couldn't find him. So, I stared at Kingston some more.

"Do you want to go talk to him?" Sadie asked.

I shook my head, despite the *yes* screaming in my skull.

Anne nudged me toward a just emptied and wiped-down table in the back of the dining room. "Sit. We're going to go get drinks and coffee, and then all three of us can agree that it's not nearly as good as yours is."

"What if it is, though?" I asked.

"It's not," Sadie said.

I was going to be waiting at least a few minutes, given the line. Perfect time to stare at Kingston while he was too busy to notice. Was that pathetic? The chubby girl stalking her crush.

The gorgeous curvy woman staring at a man who cares about her. The correction in my head was in Owen's voice.

"You're the most stunning thing in this room." This Owen voice was external, and made butterflies dance in my stomach. I looked up to find him standing next to me. "I told Kingston you'd show."

My heart slammed into my ribs so hard, I could only hear him. "You think you know me that well?" I managed to keep my voice steady anyway.

"Parts of you."

If this was Kingston, the comment would be followed by a comment about how intimately he wanted to explore more parts. "Oh?" It wasn't my best comeback, but I still didn't know how I wanted to react to them.

"We *very* briefly considered using this as a chance to give you a huge, public apology."

I hated that idea.

"We agreed you wouldn't appreciate it," Owen said. "I was surprised Kingston saw things my way."

Because Kingston had been listening when I spilled my heart and my secrets. He hadn't even hinted that he might use my past humiliations against me. The opposite, in fact. "Did he tell you why?"

"A very reasonable *taking this public forces Lyn's hand and that's wrong.*"

"He didn't tell you anything else?"

asking for it

Owen shook his head. "If you shared anything with him, it's between you and him until you tell me otherwise."

"Until. You assume—"

"Nothing," Owen said. "I'm not a *make assumptions* kind of guy."

"You assumed I'd show up here today."

"I knew you would. It's different."

I rolled my eyes. I was enjoying this so much, and it was the most basic banter. "You're an arrogant asshole."

"So, I've been told. But I knew you would be here, because if our roles were reversed, I'd have shown up. You saw what you wanted to, does that mean you're leaving?"

"Yes." Was I pleased or slightly terrified that he knew me so well?

"Give me two minutes of your time?"

I wanted to give him all my time, but there was a little catch inside. One tiny doubt that was loud enough I couldn't ignore it. I didn't want to be hurt again. Especially not by them. "I'm pretty sure you've already taken at least that much."

"Please."

"One minute."

He grabbed a napkin from the canister on the table, wrote *Reserved* on it in the most perfect block letters, and set it down.

I followed him through an *Employees Only* door, down an empty hallway that led us away from the excitement of the café.

We stepped into a back office and he closed the door behind us.

I wiggled my fingers, not sure what to do or say. "So what—"

Owen cupped my cheeks in his palms and crushed his mouth to mine. The intensity in his kiss re-broke my heart. Or maybe that was the walls around it shattering. Either way, it was the most delicious agony. Why hadn't we done more of this before? I wanted all his kisses. Forever.

I summoned what little willpower I had, and pushed him back. "I can't—" what? I didn't know what I could or couldn't do. I reached for the door.

Owen loosely. grabbed my wrist.

I could break away, but did I want to?

"I can only speak for me, because Kingston would be upset if I stole his moment," Owen said. "I'm sorry about what happened—what we did. I'd take it back. I tried, and it wasn't an option. I can apologize over and over, and do better next time, if you let me have that chance. I've never met *anyone* like you. You fill a void in my life I didn't know was there. I love you."

That was definitely my heart falling into a million pieces. "You don't get to say that to me. Not now."

"You being pissed off doesn't change how I feel, but I don't say it to manipulate you. You know me better than that."

Did I?

Yeah, I did. Damn it.

"Good luck with the new shop. Not that you need it." I reached for the door again.

This time Owen didn't stop me from leaving.

Chapter Twenty-Five

When I got back to the table, Sadie and Anne had returned with drinks and pastries.

"Got your note." Sadie held up the *Reserved* napkin. "Not your handwriting, though."

Was I flushed? Scowling? My brain and heart were a jumbled mess.

"Did you talk to Owen?" Anne asked.

I nodded.

"It went that well?" Sadie's question was a discordant blend of flat and teasing.

I shrugged. "I don't know. It wasn't bad. It was… kind of really good."

Sadie toed an empty chair toward me. "What are you doing back here?"

"I don't know. About any of it. Still." I sank into the chair. I had my answer, knew what I wanted. Why couldn't I embrace it?

Because part of me still argued I wasn't worth this kind of hassle.

But you are. I didn't know if that was Owen, Kingston, or even Sadie arguing with me.

asking for it

Damn it.

We sat and chatted. Anne and Sadie never asked if I wanted to go, but they did both feed me sweets. They had six that looked incredible—cheese, cherries, chocolate, more chocolate, mint, and a fruit tart—and insisted we had to sample all of them.

They also insisted my baking was better. They were wrong. Owen's recipes were different, but they were just as good as anything I made. I wasn't surprised or upset about the confirmation.

More than an hour passed. We were taking up valuable table space, and I didn't know what I wanted to accomplish. We should go.

"Lyn?" Kingston's voice drew my attention. He stood a few feet away, watching me with an unreadable expression. "I thought you left."

"Holy shit, Fattie Bush, Lyn, is that you?"

My gut curdled and the world around me slowed to a crawl. The new voice was one that still haunted my dreams. I looked up to see Samuel, my ex-boyfriend from school. The horror in my veins matched Sadie and Anne's expressions.

Kingston radiated a rage I'd never seen before. He followed my gaze, and in a single, fluid motion, grabbed Samuel by the collar and pinned him to a nearby wall.

"What the fuck did you just say?" Kingston growled.

Samuel held up his hands and twisted, but didn't break free. "What the fuck? This isn't about you."

"It is." Kingston drew back his free arm and landed a fist in Samuel's gut.

Samuel doubled over with a gagging gasp.

"Brutal." Sadie sounded awed.

"Sexy." So did Anne.

Humiliating. Or was it? It was definitely stupid.

Samuel stumbled away, muttering something about suing the store until it crashed and burned.

"You just destroyed your café, Day One." I wished I could be as impressed as Sadie and Anne. I was grateful, though. Was that wrong of me?

"You sound too much like Owen. I say there's no such thing as bad publicity. I have to handle this—don't leave." Kingston flashed me a smirk, and was gone.

I missed that look.

"Tell me you're not swooning at least a little on the inside," Sadie said.

I faced my friends again. "I thought you were on my side."

Anne fiddled with the paper sleeve on her coffee cup. "We are. Never doubt that. And sometimes that means telling you you're wrong. You haven't taken your eyes off him for more than a few minutes at a time. I'm surprised he snuck up on you."

"He just risked his entire store to stick up for you. Do you still think he wants anything from you besides *you*?" At least Sadie was consistent in her argument. "Do you really want to leave?"

I wanted this to be better. The hurt wouldn't magically evaporate, but I believed that Owen and Kingston were sorry. That they wanted to move forward. And Owen was right—their actions were only worth it for someone who mattered to them. None of this was worth their time unless they actually cared about me. "No."

"Sorry about that." Kingston was back, apron gone, and a baseball cap pulled low. "The leaving you alone, not the other thing. I won't apologize for shutting up that loudmouth fuck. Anyway, I need to make myself scarce. Join me?" He nodded toward the same door Owen took me through earlier.

I was out of arguments. I followed him into the empty hallway, along with Sadie and Anne.

"You're staying?" Kingston asked. "I'll drive you home."

I was staying. I turned to my friends. "I'll be okay."

Anne nodded.

Sadie stepped past me, and stopped when she was toe-to-top with Kingston. She was at least a head shorter, but she focused a frighteningly fierce glare on him. "You met Luke? The Marine?"

"I did," Kingston said.

"If you hurt Lyn again, at all, if you make her doubt anything, what Luke could do to you will pale compared to what I will." She spoke with so much assurance I didn't doubt she would make good on the threat.

I loved my friends.

"I don't doubt it for a second." Kingston was serious. "And I'd deserve it."

"Damn right you would." Sadie squeezed my hand. "Call me if you need me, Lyn."

I was smiling in spite of myself. "I will. Thank you."

Anne and Sadie left.

Kingston offered his arm. It didn't matter that we were probably only walking the short distance to the café office, I fitted my hand in the crook of his elbow. More of my doubt flitted away at how right the contact felt.

Owen was already—still?—waiting in the office, when Kingston pulled us inside and shut the door.

Kingston dropped to his knees. "I'm so sorry." He looked the way he had the day we went up to the lake. "I miss you. I want you in my life. I'd do anything in my power to make this right. Just tell me what. Jewelry? A lifetime supply of whipped cream? Beat up another ex-boyfriend?"

asking for it

After all the angst, was I going to cave so easily? "I don't want *things*."

"Neither do we," Kingston said. "But I don't know what else to offer. You stopped talking to us. I don't know how else to show you how much you matter, than to give you everything. And I would. Do you want the coffee shop?" He pulled a key ring out of his pocket, and started working one key free.

I covered his hand, biting back a whimper at the shock that raced through me. "I don't want the coffee shop."

"I want something," Owen said. "I know I don't have a right to ask, but I want it anyway."

I didn't want to guess what he'd say. "What?"

"Time. And you."

Damn it.

"That's two things," Kingston said. "I thought you were the math guy."

Was he seriously…? Of course he was. Humor to hide insecurity. The same way I used bravado to hide mine.

"I was so close to trusting you, but…" I sighed. "But I want to. Trust you. I miss you both, too, and I want us to work, but…" What?

Owen moved closer, gripping my fingers and running his thumb over my knuckles. "I'll say it over and over, we both will, and we'll keep proving this is about you. About how we feel about you, until you know it's true."

Kingston stood and gripped the back of my neck. The possession in his touch sparked through my entire body. His kiss stole my breath. My thoughts. Everything. The harder he pushed, crushing his mouth to mine, the further I fell into him.

He didn't have to do anything but kiss me, to light my senses on fire and leave me whimpering for more.

He rested his forehead against mine. "I only kiss one other person like that."

Right. They loved each other. I'd seen it with that first kiss. I heard it in the way they talked to and about each other. And they treated me the same way. "All right. I'll give you time."

"So, we're free this afternoon," Kingston murmured against my lips.

"You're not free." Every inch of my body screamed *more*. "You're opening a brand new store. You won't prove anything by walking away from the event."

"That's not what this is," Owen said. "We don't usually attend our own Grand Openings. We're only here to see you."

Kingston tugged me gently toward the door. "*As I was saying*, we've got a room in the hotel next door, so we could be up here during construction. If you'd like to come over and—"

"Wash off the non-existent coffee?" I asked.

"I was going to say *fuck*, but if we're using euphemisms now…"

I smiled. Wow, that felt good. "You have a little more wooing to do"—but not much—"before I say *yes* to sex. But *no* to the euphemisms."

"What?" Kingston sounded shocked. "You don't want my pulsating rod deep inside your love tunnel?"

I laughed.

"You'll be lucky if she wants you within ten feet of her, when you talk like that." Amusement marred Owen's serious tone.

Kingston brushed his lips over mine. "That does make me really fucking lucky, it's true."

"You're impossible." So was this entire situation. But it felt right and real. *They* felt right and real.

Twenty-Six

The walk across the parking lot, to their hotel, was agonizing. Mostly because I wanted us to have privacy.

Owen unlocked his room and let us in. The instant we were closed off from the outside world, Kingston tugged me into his arms.

I pressed a finger to his lips, and nudged him back. "I'm not that that easy, and we're not done talking yet."

He pouted and watched me with wide, puppy-dog eyes.

Disturbingly sexy.

"What would you like to talk about?" Owen sounded reasonable, but his hand was under my shirt, fingers gliding up my spine.

Talk? My brain stalled. "I… You… Before this all fell apart, we had something else to discuss." Was it smart to put this back on them? Pretty sure they only had one thing on their minds right now—me. Not that I had an issue with that.

asking for it

"Technically we already talked about that." Kingston traced a finger over my bottom lip. "We both want to be with you. In a long-term way. And in a *God, I missed you and you look amazing,* way. But to the first, we don't have a problem sharing you. How do you feel about it?"

Not the most eloquent phrasing. "Sharing me? Like I'm a pastry?"

Kingston dipped his head to trace his tongue up the side of my neck. "With extra chocolate syrup," he whispered in my ear.

Pleasant shivers raced over me.

"Dating. Seeing what comes next. Falling further," Owen said. "Three ways. Kingston and I are exploring things, too. God, I want you to be a part of it."

I did to. I wanted to melt into them and stay here forever. "I'd be hurt if you wanted otherwise, and I'm tired of hurt."

Owen spun me to face him, and cupped my face between his palms. "I'm tired of it too. We're going to make things right."

There was no hesitation or tenderness in his kiss. He dove in, devouring my mouth and my moans. Bruising my lips. Pressing in until the rest of the world fell away. I could stay wrapped in him, in them, forever.

"I promise all the teasing and foreplay next time." Owen's gravelly turned-on voice was even better in person. "But right now, I need to feel you. Tell me I can fuck you."

I wanted that too. "Yes."

When he yanked up my shirt, something ripped.

I didn't care. I loved the hunger and frantic abandon as much as I loved the way I was pressed between the two men.

Kingston's hands roamed everywhere my skin was exposed.

Owen alternated between kissing me and tearing at our clothes as though neither of us could get naked fast enough.

And then there was nothing between us. Owen's skin was hot against mine as he used his full body to push me back to the bed. He straddled my thigh, one knee between my legs, grabbed my wrists in his hand, and pinned them above my head.

This blew fantasy out of the water. Especially when he crushed his mouth to mine, and dragged a row of nibbles down my jaw, to suck on my neck. He pressed his leg higher, into me, giving me something to grind against.

Kingston knelt next to me on the bed. He'd lost his clothes, too. He cupped my breasts and flicked his thumb lightly over one nipple.

As I whimpered, an amazing reality drifted in to wrap around us. They were here with me because they liked me. Not for some fetish or just to get laid or to steal what I'd worked for.

This was my life. Not a borrowed night. Not something that would end in the morning, or later tonight, or in half an hour. I got to discover what happened next, after the incredible sex. And I already had a good idea it would be amazing.

Which made every touch that much more intense.

Owen let go of my wrists to straighten up and roll on a condom, and moved completely between my legs. My anticipation surged when he nudged my opening. I arched my back with a moan, pushing into him, when he penetrated me.

"Fuck." His groan was breathless.

There was no more build-up. He pushed my legs forward, gripping the back of my thighs, and slammed inside me at a frantic pace.

Kingston continued to devour my neck. My shoulder. My nipples.

I reached out, needing him to be more a part of this, and gripped his shaft. He adjusted to give me a better angle.

A new spark of ecstasy sped over me when Owen pressed a thumb to my clit. He pushed me to the edge, then eased back, never letting up on his thrusting.

Orgasm slammed into me, and everything shifted to vivid. The touches. Sounds. Scents. It was all high definition and all consuming.

I was still wrapped in the sharpness when Kingston pulled away. He kissed the outer shell of my ear, and whispered, "Play with your tits."

I moved my hands to my chest. Squeezing. Pinching. Tugging. Kingston knelt next to my head, cock in his fist.

"I love seeing you like this." His words were punctuated with grunts as he stroked himself. "Laid out. Flushed. Stunning and caught up in pleasure."

"Me too. I mean…" I hoped he knew what I meant.

Owen gripped my legs tighter, thumbs digging into my skin. He shifted the angle enough that each new thrust struck something deep inside. "I can't…" He panted. "You feel too good. I can't hold out."

I clenched around him in response.

I knew those staccato grunts. The fast, stuttered sound of his orgasm. That drawn out final groan before he paused, then relaxed. He resumed a lazy, out almost to the tip then back in again pace. Then slid his cock higher, to tease my clit.

I was too sensitive. It was too much. But I didn't want to pull away.

Kingston spilled a warm, sticky stream across my chest, covering me with ribbons of cum.

The sight, the moment, Owen's touch, their pleasure, drew me to climax again. This one drawing out until my entire body shuddered.

I struggled to catch my breath as I collapsed back on the mattress. Owen leaned in to kiss me. More gently this time, but it was still just as amazing. "Don't go anywhere."

Not that my legs would let me even if I wanted to.

Kingston kissed me again, everywhere. He didn't try to avoid the mess as he lightly teased his tongue over my nipples. Each lick sent another shudder through me, until I had to nudge him away.

When Owen returned, he tugged Kingston up, and crushed their mouths together. Oh, wow. The woman who walked away from that, from what they had, was an idiot. I didn't know if I wanted to whistle or groan at the ghost of sensation that rushed through me.

They broke apart, and Owen used the wet washcloth he'd fetched to gently cleaned me up. A moment later, both of them collapsed on either side of me on the bed. Owen pulled me back into him.

Kingston studied us with one eyebrow raised. "I'm going to allow it. But only because he was gone for a month, and then I got him to myself for a month after that."

"Allow it?" I let the disbelief slide into my question.

"Yes." Kingston brushed his lips over mine. "If that's all right with you."

Owen kissed along the back of my neck. "Whatever my Kitty Cat wants, she gets."

"Oh, there's got to be a story behind a nickname like that." Kingston lay on the pillow facing me, and rested a hand on my hip.

I shook my head. "It's not a great one."

"It's a fantastic one," Owen countered. "And it comes with a picture."

"I used to come with pictures," Kingston teased. "Probably won't be doing that again for a while."

I appreciated the sentiment, but didn't buy it. "You're implying you're not going to jerk off to porn anymore?"

"Is it porn of you?" Kingston's face lit up. "Or are you watching with me? I could get into that."

Owen's sigh was heavy and exaggerated, his breath caressing my back. "You're impossible some days."

Kingston smirked. "But you still love me. Go figure."

"I think you're both perfect," I said.

asking for it

"*You're* biased. But also brilliant. And right." Owen kissed my shoulder.

One phone in the room chimed, and then another seconds later. "Do you have to get that?" I wanted the answer to be *no*.

"They'll wait." Kingston didn't make any hint at moving.

And then the rings sounded again, one and then another. And again, seconds later.

"One of you should get that." I didn't want to be jostled, but it was probably urgent.

Owen kissed my bare shoulder. "Not me. Let the Punisher do it."

"Fine." Kingston rolled out of bed, and fished his jeans from the floor to grab his phone from the pocket. He jabbed the screen, then listened for a moment, before sighing. "Dylan is freaking out. Our social media manager." He looked at me. "The internet is blowing up that one of our employees assaulted a customer."

"One of your employees?" I raised my brows.

Kingston dropped back onto the bed. "There's video."

Of course there was. I frowned.

He tapped my nose playfully. "Don't look like that. I'd do the same thing again in a heartbeat." He swiped his phone again. Ringing echoed from the speaker when he set the device in the middle of the bed.

"Thank, God. It's about time you called me back. What did you do?" The woman who answered the phone sounded panicked.

I would be too.

Kingston's sigh was exaggerated. "You saw what I did. The asshole deserved it. I'm not sorry."

"You're going to give me a heart attack. Before I'm thirty. I want to live to see thirty," Dylan said.

Something told me this wasn't the first time she'd dealt with Kingston's impulsiveness. Anne and Sadie had been right earlier—I liked that it was about me this time. Was that wrong?

"We have an official company statement." Owen sounded more professional.

Dylan's laugh was strained. "Thank you. I'm listening."

Owen pursed his lips and furrowed his brow before speaking again. "While we don't condone violence, we also abhor any level of bullying or degradation. The employee in question will be disciplined, and the customer is no longer allowed in any of our establishments." He was good. "Make it sound pretty, and send it to me for approval."

"On it, Boss. Keep him on a leash for the rest of the weekend? I'm going to have my hands full with this."

asking for it

Kingston looked at us with a hungry grin. "Won't be a problem." He disconnected.

"The employee in question." I repeated Owen's phrasing, amused at the idea of anyone trying to discipline Kingston. "Would you really put him on a leash?" Could I get into that? Owen dominating Kingston? Without a doubt.

Owen shrugged. "Kingston's right that this isn't bad publicity. Some people will boycott the café. Others will come in specifically because of what he did. He'll never work there again, regardless. The leash idea does have possibility."

Kingston flopped onto his back, laying his head on my thigh. I loved everything about the casually intimate contact. "Given there's no leash in the room, does anyone want strawberry crepes?"

"They're not even in the same category, and it's six in the evening." Why was I arguing? Those sounded amazing.

"Lemon and blueberry, then." Kingston rolled to look me in the eye, never breaking contact. "You've never had breakfast for dinner?"

"More times than I care to admit." Then again, I hated admitting to anyone that I ate anything besides lettuce. It was odd for me to throw out a comment like that so casually, but I liked knowing that it was safe.

"Whatever you would like," Owen said.

I also liked knowing he meant that. "Crepes sound wonderful." In fact, all of this was wonderful. I meant what I told them about wanting time to rebuild trust, but my heart had already surrendered, and I was pretty confident they'd be gentle with it.

"When you smile like that, it looks whimsical. I love that look," Kingston said.

Me too.

Owen sat, and pulled me upright too, so I was leaning against him. "Care to share what you're thinking?" he said.

What was I thinking, besides *hehe, sexy men like me*. I forced my thoughts to assemble.

"The night I met *Fred* and *Barney*, I was a heartbeat away from a pity party, because my friends were drifting away from me, to be with their men, and I was going to be alone forever."

Kingston opened his mouth.

I silenced him with a look, before he could deny or correct past me's assumptions. "Turns out I never lost them. And now I have my two guys, too. Life is pretty freaking amazing."

"It really is." Owen brushed his lips over mine.

I glanced at Kingston. "You were saying?"

asking for it

"Nothing you didn't already. You do have us, eating out of your hand… off your stomach… licking everywhere…" He rattled his head. "And it's fucking incredible."

And it would only get better. I had no doubt.

Epilogue

Six Months Later

A pair of kisses was my favorite way to wake up in the morning, and today was no exception. It was the perfect way to drift into a new day.

Owen and Kingston were wavering on long-term housing, so they were still living the hotel life, and still sharing a room. But most nights all three of us ended up in the same place. Last night though, they showered me with kisses and apologies and told me they had things to take care of early.

I'd been bummed, but I trusted them. Completely. It was an amazing feeling.

I finally let my eyes flutter open, to them on either side of me. They were fully clothed compared to my flimsy T-shirt and panties. That hardly seemed fair. "I thought you were busy."

"We are. Get dressed." Kingston defied his own words by draping an arm over my stomach. "I'd say wear that, because yummy, but we're going out."

"Out where?" I wasn't motivated to move anyway, pressed between two warm bodies, but even less so if a surprise was involved.

Owen stood and tugged my hand. "Vacation."

I couldn't go on vacation. "I have too much work." There was planning to do. Schedules to rearrange—

"Taken care of." Owen was probably as good as reading my mind. He brushed his lips over my fingertips. "You have to let this happen sometime."

Kingston rolled to the side and stood, before taking my other hand. "Everything will be fine."

In the past few months I'd hired another baker and a few more café employees. I'd taken test days off, and things could run on their own. Violet was more than competent. But the idea of walking away from my baby for more than a day terrified me.

They were right. Time to dive in. I forced myself from bed. "What do I need to pack?" I asked as dressed. It had taken time to get used to being in various stages of undress around them, but now it felt natural.

"Taken care of," Owen repeated. "Sadie came by while you were working yesterday.

"Already taken care of," Owen repeated. "Sadie came by while you were working yesterday."

I pursed my lips. "You're making me regret giving you keys."

"No we're not. You ready?" Kingston said. "I swear you won't regret this. I wouldn't do that to you. We wouldn't."

"All right." I wasn't really ready, but they were going to talk me into it eventually.

My world went black when a blindfold was fitted over my eyes. "Uh…"

I could navigate my house, including the up and down, on a pitch black night with my eyes closed, but I was still nervous letting them lead me downstairs. Kingston held my hand until I was seated in a vehicle. Owen's Jeep based on the height, and the faint scent of *New Car* air freshener.

The three of us talking was a nice distraction as Owen drove, but it didn't erase my anxiousness. Each time I reached for the blindfold, one of them grabbed my hand.

The car stopped, and the engine shut off.

"Now you can look." Kingston pulled away the blindfold.

We were in a parking garage. From the signs outside the window, it was long-term airport parking.

"Okay…?" I wasn't surprised by this bit, since Sadie had packed my bags, and it was too cold for camping. Besides, Owen didn't like roughing it any more than I did.

"Kingston wanted to keep things a surprise until we landed. At our final destination," Owen said. "But changing planes, taking you through customs, and everything else required, all without you figuring things out or anyone asking questions… Let's just say even I couldn't figure out that logic."

"Customs?" Where were we going?

Kingston handed me a boarding pass. "Tokyo."

My heart did a happy little jump skip. "Really? I mean, duh, of course, the ticket says so, but… really?" I'm glad I didn't put up more of a fight this morning. So many firsts about to happen, both terrifying and exciting. *Tokyo*. "You've been planning this for months," I realized. Now I knew why Owen insisted I get a passport.

He shrugged. "Guilty."

They unloaded the luggage from the back of the Jeep, refusing to let me carry any of it. If anyone besides Sadie had packed for me, I'd insist on checking everything before we went any farther, but she probably had me more than prepared.

There were only a couple of other people on the shuttle to the airport. Owen tangled his fingers with mine as he sat next to me.

Kingston was on my other side, and kept an arm wrapped around me. "Odds of joining the Mile-High Club?" he asked in a soft, playful voice.

I loved the idea, but it also scared me. I wasn't sure I was there yet. "Ask me again on the trip home."

"I will. Believe it." Kingston kissed me on the cheek.

We reached Terminal 1, checked our luggage, made it through security without any hassle, and grabbed coffee before reaching our gate.

With caffeine pumping through my veins, and some of my excitement settling, my brain was firing on all cylinders again. I had a surprise for them, too. I'd been saving it for our six-month anniversary, but that was only a few days off, so telling them now was just as good.

I never imagined I'd be the person who celebrated every relationship milestone, but we'd made a big deal out of every month together, and it hadn't gotten old yet.

Then again, everything about our relationship was still fresh and amazing.

"I need to show you something." I grabbed my phone and scrolled through images.

Kingston rested his chin on my shoulder. "Dirty pictures?"

"Seductively sweet pictures?" Owen asked.

"Both." Not really. At least, not at all in the way they meant. "I've been thinking…" Now that the words were on my lips, it felt like a presumptuous assumption. But I trusted them. I knew what we had, and how real it was.

The reminder was enough to propel me forward. I showed them my screen. It was a mock-up of the Loading Java logo—the brunette perched on the edge of the coffee cup—but she wore their crown. "I know I only bring my shop to the table, and my recipes, but—"

"Yes." Kingston cut me off.

"Only if we're completely equal partners," Owen added. "You have as much say in any decision as we do."

"But only if we get your recipes. You did say that. Promise me." Kingston's voice was light.

I couldn't hide my smile. "I did say that."

Kingston twitched in his seat, half standing, then sitting again.

"Do you need to pee or something?" Owen asked.

Kingston rolled his eyes and flipped Owen off. "I want to go down on one knee," Kingston said. "But… public."

My smile grew. "I'd be okay with it, just this once, but only because you warned me."

Kingston dropped to one knee in front of me. I'd seen this twice before, but this time he wasn't apologizing. He grasped my fingers. "You're my universe. I love you more than anyone, and I every day I thank any god who listens that I found you. I can't imagine not having you in my life. Our life.

You're the perfect addition. Nothing would make me—us—happier than to call you partner in everything. Business. Life."

My breath caught. This was half a heartbeat from… "You almost make it sound like you're proposing."

"I'm not. Not yet. That's the next surprise, two nights from now at the base of Mt Fuji."

I caught my laugh when I studied his face and saw how serious he was. "Now it's not a surprise."

Kingston shrugged. "You don't like surprises."

"If you're not asking yet, I'll save my *yes* until then." I looked at Owen. "Does he speak for you?"

Owen gave me a half smile. "Only sometimes. He's more eloquent and personable than me, so I'm just going to kiss you and remind you that you and I love each other, so this makes perfect sense."

"It really does." I brushed my lips over Owen's, then leaned forward to kiss Kingston. "I love you both so much."

A small smatter of claps erupted around us, and I flushed that we'd drawn a small audience. I had no idea what anyone thought of the fact I was kissing both men, but screw anyone else's opinions.

"You can stand now," I murmured to Kingston.

His grin grew. "I know. But one of my favorite things is being on my knees at your feet."

"Get up ." I tugged him to his feet with a laugh.

asking for it

This was more amazing than I ever thought I'd have. Than I even believed I deserved, a year ago. I was excited for Tokyo, this business partnership, and spending the rest of my life with these two incredible men.

Epilogue Two

Owen

I'd had as many lows as highs in my life, but the notable highs soared above anything else. Meeting Kingston. Meeting Lyn. Watching their joy and awe and excitement as we touched down in Tokyo.

Together, it was hard to argue with them when they wanted to see the city *now* instead of sleeping first. But the fact that Lyn couldn't stop yawning as she insisted she was fine, because she'd slept on the plane, made it easy for me to veto.

Touring the city with them was incredible. Tokyo was on my bucket list anyway, but it was that much better seeing it through their eyes.

As the sun crept lower in the sky, Kingston was checking his phone more and more often. Sexy, fidgety fucker.

"Do you have something else you'd rather be doing?" Lyn asked playfully after check number twenty-seven.

asking for it

Kingston pocketed his phone. "I was thinking… sleep off this jet lag some more? Or at least back to our place, and rest for a few hours."

This was as close to subtlety as he got. I adored it. Since he gave his *let's be together forever* speech in the airport, I'd convinced him to let me do the talking once we got back to our rental.

"I could rest for a few hours." *Rest.* As if that was going to happen.

Lyn looked between us with a smile. "I already know what's going to happen. You already know what I'm going to say."

Kingston slipped one hand into hers and one into mine. "But it's not official until it *does* happen."

"I agree." Besides, I had a surprise still—one I suspected Lyn would be okay with—that carried the weight of a second ring nestled away in my luggage.

Lyn's sigh was exaggerated. "All right. Let's go back, so I can find out what this big not-surprise is that you're proposing."

I shook my head at her word choice, but mostly because I didn't think of it first.

We'd opted to rent a more traditional guest house rather than a hotel room. When we stepped inside, Lyn's mouth fell open. "Wow." Her voice was soft as she took it all in.

It was as beautiful in person as online, but I was more interested in watching her as she explored every room, through sliding doors, to discover the futon in the bedroom, her attention lingering on stunning inked artwork.

While she and Kingston explored, I took the excuse to slip a box with two rings into my pocket.

"It's amazing." Lyn finally looked at me.

I couldn't see anything else. "Yeah, you are."

Pink flushed her cheeks. I loved that look on her. I loved any look on her.

Lyn ducked her head. "If you're not careful, I might start to like surprises."

"You're going to love this one. I promise." I grasped her fingers and tugged her closer.

"This one's not really a surprise, though."

If I wasn't careful, I'd break my stern façade too soon. "Trust me."

Kingston watched us both with a sexy smirk that said he had answers no one else did. Time to prove him wrong. I cupped his cheek and held his gaze. The warmth and affection that looked back was tinged with a hint of shock, and took my breath away.

"Every day, I'm grateful I met you," I said to Kingston. "It took me longer than I should have to figure it out, but I've loved you for years. You're my opposite. The perfect partner in everything. My best friend."

"And I keep you from being wound too tight." His playful retort caught.

I smiled. "And that." I turned to Lyn, drawing her fingers up to kiss the tips. "And you. You're sunshine, you're warmth, you're so much I need that I never knew I was missing. You compliment both of us. I can't imagine not knowing you. Not having you in my life—our lives. Because I can't imagine there not being an *us* that involves you, me, and Kingston."

This wasn't what I'd planned to say, but as happened frequently, I had to adapt when one of them turned big, adoring eyes on me. I had to let go of both of them to tug the rings free, but it wasn't enough time to regather my thoughts.

"I don't care what we call what we have, as long as there's a promise of forever. I want—need—you both in my life." I opened the box.

Lyn clapped and squealed with delight. "Yes. That's what I'm supposed to say, right? Because *yes*. Always yes."

"You sneaky bastard," Kingston said. "Me too."

I raised an eyebrow. "You have to say it."

"Yes." His smirk was back.

I slipped Lyn's ring on her finger first. The bands were both simple, black titanium. "Anne helped me size it. We can pick something more vibrant if you want."

"I don't want. It's perfect." Lyn threw her arms around my neck and kissed me hard. Her body molded to mine, the perfect amount of soft and yielding mixed with insistence. Just like her.

When Kingston cleared his throat, I let Lyn go and turned to him. "Feeling left out?" I teased.

"I want a ring too." He held out his left hand, ring finger isolated.

I slipped his band into place, dropped the box, and gripped the back of his neck, holding him captive.

His grunt of surprise was intoxicating. I crushed my mouth to his and dove my tongue past his lips to dance and tease around his tongue. Sparks practically sizzled from us. I was so glad I'd stopped denying what this was.

When I finally let Kingston go, he stood there for a moment, eyes half shut and mouth half open. He shook his head and turned to Lyn. "Me too. I already gave my pretty speech. But you, me, all of us. Partners in everything?"

"Yes. Of course. Always." Lyn nodded.

Watching them kiss was as delicious as participating. An incredible blend of chaos and beauty, wrapped around each other. It was enough to make me hard.

Lyn gripped Kingston's fingers and mine when they broke apart. "I want to ask something too." Her tone was shy. Seductive.

"Anything." As if I could deny her.

asking for it

Her blush was back. "I want to watch the two of you celebrate your engagement."

Because she loved to see me with Kingston, and always flushed when she asked. "We can do that."

———

Kingston

I'd never looked too closely at my relationship with Owen. Digging past the surface, to the shared hook-ups, the sex even when there wasn't another person there, was the kind of thing that could end friendships.

I didn't dare do that.

Then Lyn came along…

And now here I was, on my knees, with my best friend's cock in my mouth, while our girlfriend watched.

I'd never been so turned on. Submitting this way, tasting Owen, and hearing Lyn's gasps.

I was surprised when Owen pulled back. He tugged me to my feet, and gripped my chin. The possession in his gaze stopped my heart.

"*God*, I want to fuck you." His voice was low and commanding.

I nodded toward our luggage. "You know where the lube is."

I stripped off my clothes and crawled toward Lyn, who had her shirt and bra pushed out of the way and was watching with her tongue caught between her teeth. I absolutely got off on her getting off on watching us.

Her eyes grew wide, and I was stalled by Owen's hand on my throat. He pulled me upright, so I was kneeling, back pressed into his chest.

"I'm not done with you." He growled.

Fuck. Here I thought I couldn't get any harder. I was pretty sure Owen secretly delighted in proving me wrong, even when he didn't know what I was thinking.

Owen bit my shoulder and I groaned at the sting. Desire screamed though me. Every muscle in my body tensed in anticipation.

I grunted in surprise when the cold lube hit my skin, but I adjusted quickly as Owen glided slippery fingers along my ass. He teased my opening, penetrating just enough to taunt me.

My dick stood at attention and begged for the same. I was willing to drag out the agony a little longer, to make this last.

Owen pressed his other palm into the small of my back, urging me forward, until I was on all fours again.

He inched his cock inside me. We'd done this enough that relaxing was second nature, and the anticipation of the tight fit, of being stretched out, cranked my pulse to full speed.

The futon shifted, drawing my attention to Lyn. She wriggled out of her pants and stripped off her shirt, not taking her gaze off us for more than a few seconds at a time. I loved that sight. The rise and fall of her chest. The flush in her skin and gleam on her lips as she licked them.

I was torn between using both hands to support myself, and reaching for my cock, where it hung aching to be touched.

When Owen reached around to grip my shaft, I groaned at his possessive touch. He yanked hard. Fast. As if demanding I enjoy the moment. And I did. My breath came in short pants as he pumped me fast, but rocked inside me slowly.

Lyn slid three fingers inside herself, dropping her other hand to play with her clit. She was as captivating as she was captivated, making me wonder where to focus. Especially when those intoxicating whimpers started falling past her lips.

Owen moved his hands to my hips, gripping hard and pounding harder. He was done holding back, which means his patience had run out.

Was I smug about that? About pushing him to the point where physical gratification was his core goal? Damn right I was.

But I was out of patience too. I fisted my own cock, choking and stroking. Faster. Harder. In time with Owen's thrusts. Spurred by Lyn's mewls. My body tensed at the sensory overload, and reveled in it.

My balls tightened. Stars danced behind my eyes. Pressure built inside and release hovered just out of reach.

And then Lyn made the amazing gasping sound that meant she was coming. Her face screwed up. Her hand moved at high speed. Fuck, she was gorgeous when she was lost in climax.

I came hard, shudders racking my body. Jizz coated my hand and splattered the blanket. I didn't want to stop, especially with Owen still buried in me, but my energy faded as skin became hyper-sensitive.

Owen's grip tightened. He was going to leave marks. Good. His grunts were louder than Lyn's. Roars of ecstasy in the open room. His rhythm increased to high speed, then stuttered to a stop.

He kissed along my spine as he pulled me upright, and reached around to cup my softening cock. The *mine* in his touch was implied.

And I was. I belonged to him. To her. The three of us were incomplete without each other.

We cleaned up, changed the comforter, and collapsed in a pile on the futon. Lyn buried her face in my chest, and Owen draped an arm over me, pinning me in place.

This was status quo for us, and I had no complaints. "So, when we get home... house shopping?" I liked sharing a room with Owen, but I was tired of living in a hotel. I was even more tired of those nights when Lyn ended up in a different place than us.

"Are you going to buy me a nice one?" she asked.

I loved that she was comfortable asking. "Whatever you want."

"Hmm…" Her consideration hummed against my skin. "I kind of like where I am."

I would have made a face, but she wouldn't see it.

"Kind of?" Owen asked.

She kissed my chest. "Okay, a lot. It's near my friends. I know it's not big or grand, but it's mine. It could be ours."

So much for giving in easily to us buying her something huge.

"It doesn't have to be grand, as long as we're all there." Of course Owen had to be reasonable.

I let out an exaggerated sigh. "I don't know if you're being sappy, or just yourself."

"Both. Are we talking about moving into Lyn's place?"

Lyn rolled away enough that she could see me and past me to Owen. "It's a little cramped for billionaire life."

"Pretty sure I offered to fix that." New place. Huge house.

Owen squeezed my hip. "The property next to yours is for sale." Of course he knew that.

I liked the idea. "It's a longer commute, but not by much." I studied Lyn. "You don't have to decide tonight, but we're not going anywhere without you."

She grinned. "Damn right, you're not."

I kissed her nose, and leaned back into Owen. This was so perfect, and I was so fucking lucky. To have Lyn. To have Owen. For all of it.

About Allyson Lindt

USA Today Bestselling Author Allyson Lindt is a full-time geek and a fuller-time author. She's found her own happily ever after, where she and her spouse call their furbabies their children. Coffee is her task-master and random tangents are her muse. When she's not writing, she's fangirling over the latest superhero movies. She likes her stories with sweet geekiness and heavy spice, and loves a sexy happily-ever-after. Because cubicle dwellers need love too. Learn more about Allyson's books, including signing up for her newsletter, by visiting http://www.allysonlindt.com.